Ken + Dorothy

From

CC

aka

SR

RETRIBUTION ON ICE

Jack Rowles

authorHOUSE®

AuthorHouse™
1663 Liberty Drive
Bloomington, IN 47403
www.authorhouse.com
Phone: 1 (800) 839-8640

This is a work of fiction. All of the characters, names, incidents, organizations, and dialogue in this novel are either the products of the author's imagination or are used fictitiously.

Published by AuthorHouse   10/27/2015

ISBN: 978-1-5049-5422-8 (sc)
ISBN: 978-1-5049-5421-1 (e)

Print information available on the last page.

Any people depicted in stock imagery provided by Thinkstock are models, and such images are being used for illustrative purposes only.
Certain stock imagery © Thinkstock.

This book is printed on acid-free paper.

Because of the dynamic nature of the Internet, any web addresses or links contained in this book may have changed since publication and may no longer be valid. The views expressed in this work are solely those of the author and do not necessarily reflect the views of the publisher, and the publisher hereby disclaims any responsibility for them.

To Trixie and the twins...

Contents

Chapter 1
The Thick Blue Line

Harvey "Hunter" Hunt stood frozen, glaring at the large flat-screen TV. A short bulldog of a man, his eyes were fixed and his lips were pursed. With his fists clenched at his side, he was motionless for a full minute.

"Let's have another look at that penalty."

The screen showed a slow-motion replay of a hockey player being blindsided and pulled down to the ice. "Abbot's in the slot ready to shoot, the goalie's way out of position, and Delorme out and out just plain tackles him."

His shaved head had turned pink. You could almost see smoke coming out of his ears.

"No question about it," the color commentator said. "The refs are reluctant to call penalties in overtime. They don't want to be a factor, but even in this game-seven, sudden-death overtime, something as blatant as that has to be called. He saved what would have been a sure goal and the end of this historic series."

Had Harvey not been in his friend's basement, he would have already put his fist through the wall.

"And what a series it has been," the announcer replied. "We're running out of clichés to describe it. The Montreal Canadiens and the Toronto Maple Leafs meeting in the final for the first time since '67. Game seven. Overtime. Truly one of the greatest if not *the* greatest rivalry in all sport."

"Not only historic but also one of the best displays of play-off hockey we've seen in several years," said the color commentator. "Toronto takes a two-game lead. Montreal comes back with three straight. Toronto ties it up Thursday night. Now we're down to this."

On the nearby patio, freakishly tall Norman "Zed" Zemlak paced angrily. He paused for a second, took three measured strides, and kicked a perfect field goal sending a plastic garden gnome with a high arc and slight backspin over the rail, past the pool, and between the two tall cedars at the far end of the yard.

"Well, this Montreal crowd obviously doesn't like that penalty, and they've showered the ice with debris. It'll take a few minutes to clear it before we can get going again. The Leafs have to be so close right now that they can almost taste it, almost feel it. For most of the third period and now in overtime, they've had the Canadiens on their heels." The announcer raised his voice over the crowd noise. "And they have come oh so close with a couple of excellent opportunities that just couldn't quite find the net." He paused while the excited din of the crowd rose behind him. "The Stanley Cup is in the building, down at ice level."

The screen showed the tall, gleaming trophy guarded by two Royal Canadian Mounted Police officers in full-dress uniform of red serge jackets, Stetsons, and riding pants. The camera zoomed in on the inscription: "Dominion Hockey Challenge Cup—From Stanley of Preston." The camera was in soft focus, and the arena lights were behind it, giving it a genuine halo. "Tonight, one of these two great teams will drink champagne from Lord Stanley's Mug, that most historic piece of silverware."

"The Canadiens are clearly showing signs of fatigue at this point," said the commentator, also raising his voice. "If anything, I think they're feeling more pressure playing at home than they would if this game were in Toronto. Montreal fans are notorious for having very high expectations for their teams. Mind you, that's probably nothing when you compare it to the pressure these Leafs must be feeling."

The announcer interrupted. "Not since 1967 have these Leafs held the cup. Toronto fans have waited a long, long time for that downtown ticker-tape parade. And over these past forty-odd years, they've never been closer than they are right now."

"We're going to find out if the Canadiens have enough juice to kill off one more penalty and keep their hopes alive."

They were silent for several seconds while the cameras panned the crowd—the shirtless, drunken diehards in the cheap seats with "Go Habs" painted on their stomachs; men in dark suits with expensive rink-side seats, still and straight-faced, looking as if they were in court waiting to hear a jury's verdict. Groups of attractive young women, many of them players' wives or girlfriends. Quick shots of the two coaches pacing behind their benches, chewing gum furiously. Even a baby no more than a few months old sound asleep in his mother's arms while she stood behind the glass screaming at her team.

"And we're ready to resume play. Face-off in front of the Canadiens' net," the announcer said in a raspy voice. "Toronto wins the face-off. Nakoney swipes it back to Unger just inside the blue line ... Unger across to Thompson ... Thompson holds it for a second ... Back to

Unger. Leafs being patient ... Taking their time. Waiting. Trying to set up their shot."

"This is really smart play on the Leafs' part—" the commentator tried to insert before he was abruptly cut off.

"Pittman skates in slowly ... puts it across to Unger ... Unger down to Nakoney ... Nakoney passes across to ... It's intercepted! Sullivan steals the puck, splits the defenders ... past the blue line ... he's got LaFlamme open on the left wing! A two-man breakaway! He's too far ahead ... into the Leaf zone ... Sullivan to LaFlamme ... Scores!"

"Assholes," said Ian, the host of the evening's event as he backed up the digital video recorder a few seconds.

"He's got LaFlamme open on the left wing! A two-man breakaway! He's too far ahead ... into the Leaf zone ... Sullivan to LaFlamme ... Scores!"

"Stupid assholes!"

The machine backed up again. "He's too far ahead ... into the Leaf zone ... Sullivan to LaFlamme ... *Scores!*"

The recording continued to run. "Laurent LaFlamme ... a short-handed goal ... unbelievable ... and the Montreal Canadiens ... have won ... the Stanley Cup," said the announcer, his voice just one level below an undignified yelp. "Game seven, sudden-death overtime, and a short-handed goal! Un-be-*leeve*-a-ble!"

Hunter still stood frozen. His face was beet-red. He desperately wanted to reach through the television and grab the referee by the throat.

The commentator tried to speak up. "I don't know." He sounded concerned. "I'm not sure that shouldn't have been—"

The announcer continued shouting, oblivious to what his color man was trying to say. "Eighty-two regular-season games, twenty-three play-off games, eight months, two historic franchises, and now this."

The camera panned the crowd again. Those in the cheap seats were hugging and pouring beer over each other's heads. The suits were hugging and doing high-fives. The wives and girlfriends were hugging and crying. The baby was awake and screaming as his mother jumped up and down, ignoring him. Fireworks went off. Balloons went up while confetti and streamers rained on the ice.

"Tell your mom I owe her a new leprechaun," Zed said, returning to the room.

The color commentator's voice was drowned out by the televised crowd noise. "I think … I think they should have a look at that." More noise. "I don't think his skate touched the blue line. I think that should've been an offside. I think LaFlamme was offside. That goal should come back."

"Yeah, you're damn right," Ian concurred with the television. "I think we should have a look at that! By all means let's have a look at that! Here, I'll help you out." He used the remote control as a pointer on the frozen picture. "Look—there's his skate, there's the line. That white stuff in there is ice, you stupid sons of bitches." He yelled at the TV, "Skate … line … ice! Skate … line … ice! You could drive a bloody Zamboni through there!"

"Prick refs," said Hunter, still frozen in a semi-catatonic state. "They're asshole prick French refs. That's the problem. Prick French refs."

Ian Andrews, Harvey Hunt (whose name had morphed simply to Hunter due to his personality and outlook on life), and Norman Zemlak watched the game in the plush family room of Ian's parents' house. They were in a state of shock as if they had just received news of a death in the family.

Five minutes previously, their world had come to a halt. Sisyphus had spent more than forty years rolling one particular rock up the hill. It had never been that close to the top. It was only a few inches away. But the ground suddenly gave way, and down it tumbled again.

It was not simply the disappointment of their favorite team losing a championship. It was devastating. The monkey—a big, ugly, smelly monkey twice their age—retained its firm grip on their backs.

7

Six minutes previously, the Maple Leafs had been an angel's whisper away from winning their first Stanley Cup since 1967. It had been a long, long drought for one of the marquee teams in the league.

Their confidence in game seven had been bolstered by the fact that Montreal was to start its second-string rookie goalie in his first play-off game ever. The starter had been pulled late in game six after his fragile self-confidence was shattered by letting in three goals in a five-minute span in the third period. That night, the Canadiens looked tired from the face-off while the Leafs looked confident. They had played a controlled game and had kept their emotions in check. They had been neither too reckless nor too cautious, neither too aggressive nor subdued. They had been relaxed, in a groove, and had simply gone about taking care of business.

They had been relieved to be playing the last game in Montreal. Each team had already won on the opponent's ice. But more important, the psychic anxiety of twenty-two thousand fans holding back forty-plus years of pent-up frustration might have telepathically short-circuited the whole outfit. They were quite happy to have the Canadiens carry the pressure of the hometown crowd.

Montreal had had a two-goal lead at the end of the first period, but the Leafs had stayed calm and had come back to tie it by the end of the second. Montreal had scored again with five minutes left in the third, but Toronto had tied it again in less than sixty seconds. Momentum had clearly shifted in their favor. The Habs showed the frustration of a team unable to protect a lead compounded by the trepidation of having a rookie in the net. They hadn't been able to stick that final dagger into the Leafs' heart. They had panicked, made mental mistakes, and taken dumb penalties while the Leafs had been cool, calm, and collected and had just tried to get the job done.

Wave after wave of offensive plays, of great shots that just missed. One clanged off the post, another off the crossbar. Two miraculous saves by the Canadiens' rookie goalie. But it was just a matter of time. The Canadiens ran around swatting out little fires with their sticks while the Leafs started to turn up their flamethrowers. The gods of hockey were starting to grin. Stars were aligning themselves neatly. It was just a matter of time …

The sick feeling in their stomachs was now real. The goal shouldn't have counted, but it would. The realization sunk in. It was over. The results would not change.

Ian, Hunter, and Zed were three men in their early twenties living in Oakville, a Toronto suburb. They lived and loved the Leafs, the most important thing in their otherwise aimless lives. They attended as many games as they could afford. Being the young fools they were, they drank heavily before, after, and during the games. If they had been born British soccer fans instead of Toronto Maple Leaf fans, they would have been branded hooligans and likely would have done some jail time by then.

They were among the hundreds of thousands of people not only in Toronto but scattered throughout the country who were obsessively dedicated to the team. The inane thing about Leaf fans was that despite the team's long record of mediocrity, they continued to parade like lemmings to the box office year in, year out, and games almost always sold out. The prevailing theory was that the team was so financially successful there was no incentive for the owners to spend the money it would take to put a winning product on the ice. It was very difficult to make a business case for winning the Stanley Cup. It might make the fans happier, but it would do very little for an already fat bottom line. Whether it was an exhibition game, the season opener, a rare play-off game, or the last game of a hopeless season, seats were always hard to come by.

In 1841, a classic study of human nature with the self-explanatory title "Extraordinary Popular Delusions and the Madness of Crowds" was published. When it is revised for modern times, there will undoubtedly be a chapter examining Toronto Maple Leaf fans.

Ian, Hunter, and Zed will be the definitive case study.

Chapter 2
Clear the Benches

"And I quote from the Official Rule Book of the National Hockey League page twenty-eight rule number seventy-four, 'The position of the player's skates and not that of his stick shall be the determining factor in all instances in deciding an offside.'"

The word *offside* was spoken slowly and clearly and followed by a two-second pause.

"A player is offside when both skates are completely over the outer edge of the determining center line or blue line involved in the play."

Vaughn Tedesco, host of the morning show at station CTTR-Toronto Talk Radio ranted painfully into his microphone. "A player is *onside* when either of his skates is in contact with or on his own side of the line at the instant—" Again a pause. "—the instant the puck completely crosses the outer edge of that line.

"And my friends, as we have all clearly seen on last night's replay and on the front page of the *Star* and the *Globe and Mail* and the *National Post* and *nearly*—" He stressed the work emphatically. "—every other paper in the country—the *Montreal Gazette* and *LaPresse oddly*—" He put sarcasm into the word. "—being two of the exceptions. Yes my friends, even the *New York Times* has shown this very photo at the bottom corner of its front page."

Ian had just woken up from a disjointed sleep. He lay in bed, somewhat hungover. His eyes were half-open. He listened to his radio.

"Larry the Flame—" Laurent LaFlamme's name was often anglicized somewhat derisively. "—was *offside!* Neither of his skates was touching the blue line as per rule number seventy-four of the Official Rule Book. The play should have been called, the whistle should have been blown, the goal should have been called back. But instead of blowing their whistles, the refs blew the call, they blew the game, they blew the series. And in my humble opinion, they blew the whole darn season." The announcer paused. "Anyway you look at it, any camera angle, offside! I don't care about the pressure of the

moment. Offside! I don't care about the hometown crowd
or the fans or the virtual deluge of stuff that showered
the ice after the goal. Offside! What more can I say, my
friends?" asked the radio host. "There it is. Let's open the
phones. I think it's going to be a long show."

As he lay in bed half-awake, his mind switched
back and forth between the previous day's nightmare
and the general pointlessness his adult life had been
thus far. Almost five years ago to the day, Ian had been
valedictorian at his high school graduation. He was an
average guy of average height with average looks and
average athletic ability. He considered himself to be
sort of an intellect, a thinker, and his ambition was to
study—well, he wasn't sure what, but to study and learn
and go on to be an even greater thinker. But despite his
intellectual aspirations, he had a difficult time coming
up with a speech that was little more than the standard,
boilerplate graduation address about the future being
ours, let's change the world, let's pursue our dreams, blah,
blah, blah. It was all such crap.

After high school, he enrolled at the University
of Toronto. At first, he wanted to study some of the
more esoteric, pure sciences such as astrophysics or
quantum mechanics, but he soon realized he didn't have
the intellectual fortitude to handle the math. He thus
waded into a pool of humanities, social sciences, and

other "subjects for soft heads," as his father put it. He was in the fifth year of a four-year program, a mixed bag of anthropology, history, political science, philosophy, psychology, theology, sociology, English, and Russian literature and classics. Ian still hoped that if he exposed himself to the great subjects of Western civilization, something might eventually click and fall into place.

Ian pointedly didn't study the French. Not their literature, history, or language despite the significant role they had played in Western civilization. It occurred to him that morning that his dislike of all things French might actually have been rooted in his outright hatred of the Canadiens and their years of oppression of his beloved Leafs. A simple hockey rivalry tainted his views on an entire culture going all the way back to Louis XIV.

"Would it kill you to take a few classes with at least some semblance of practical applications?" his father had once asked him. "Economics? Accounting? Even law is still considered a respectable trade in many circles." He was an upper-midlevel cog somewhere in the bowels of one of the big banks somewhere in the canyons of downtown Toronto. He didn't have any overachieving aspirations for his son and never pressured him academically or in any other way for that matter. He thought Ian might make a fine cog himself someday if nothing else came up. "The only 'ology you're not taking is mixology. At least you'd get a job as a bartender while you're musing on the meaning of life."

Ian still carried the scars of a perfect childhood and comfortable upbringing. He'd experienced no hardships, no challenges, no victories, or no accomplishments. If, as the saying goes, the hotter the fire, the stronger the steel, his mettle would have all the characteristics of aluminum foil.

His life path seemed to point to a few more years of undergraduate mush, a master's degree in something useless, and eventually a long career as an insurance adjuster or university administrator. If he was really lucky, maybe even as a lecturer in one of the archaic subjects he'd become an expert on. He had no bloody clue as to where his life was going; maybe it wasn't too late to go to "cog" school after all.

"Well, I'm as sick as anybody, Vaughn," said the caller. "The refs obviously blew the call, but put yourself in their position. From the time they crossed the blue line and the goal light came on, how long was that? I mean as soon as the goal is scored *kapow!* You know, the whole place goes nuts, the ice is covered in garbage, both teams clear the benches—"

"What are you trying to say?" the announcer asked.

"Well, if I'm the ref in the biggest game of the year and someone scores and the whole place goes nuts in a nanosecond, what would you do? Me and the other two are supposed to tell twenty thousand Frenchies to sit down and shut up 'cause that goal didn't count? Not a chance, man. You'd get your head handed to you. They don't pay me enough for that."

"You make an interesting point," the announcer said. "Under those particular circumstances, that would be quite a task to handle."

"Hey, I recorded the game and replayed the ending about a hundred times," the caller said. "I mean, as soon as that goal light came on, the second, that very instant, all that stuff—the fireworks and balloons and that other crap—was all over the place. Man, someone sure had an itchy trigger finger. It's not the fans. Some flunky who works for the team has to push the button."

"Let's face it," said the next caller. "If you're a star in this league, you get special treatment. If it had been Joe Blow and Bobby Schmuck on that breakaway, *tweet!* You're offside. But the Flame and those guys, they get a different set of rules. And it happens in all the pro sports. In the NBA, you're allowed only two steps in a layup, but Michael Jordan usually got four or five. In baseball, when the big stars are up at bat, the strike zone is the size of a postage stamp!"

"Yeah, one of your earlier callers said that if you're a superstar, you get special treatment. Well, man, that's not even the half of it. There's favoritism built into every sport," the next caller declared. "I'll state the obvious. The NHL doesn't want one let alone two Canadian teams in the finals. It's bad for their TV ratings."

"Go on," Tedesco said.

"And what's worse is that the government doesn't want Toronto to win either. There's an election coming up, and they need votes in Quebec."

"Well, there's no shortage of opinions today," the announcer said sarcastically. "Line two, go ahead."

"Everyone who's called in today is forgetting one thing," the caller said. "Even if the Flame had been called offside and they took that goal back, the game would still have just been tied. Montreal could have just as easily gone on and—"

The radio host cut him off before he could finish the sentence.

Chapter 3
The Great Canadian Kumbaya

The five stages of grief are generally recognized as denial, anger, bargaining, depression, and acceptance in that order. What Ian, Hunter, and Zed had experienced was without question grief, but none of the stages followed in the order prescribed. As soon the goal was scored, there was anger followed by denial and back to anger and denial. The oscillation continued for more than a week overlaid with a veneer of depression. Bargaining was not an option unless of course they could get their hands on the asshole refs. Many years down the road, even after they had breathed their last and were being laid to rest in the cold, cold earth, they would never acknowledge acceptance of this tragedy.

They went over and over it in their minds. They dwelled on how painfully close they had come to ending what seemed like an eternal drought only to be disappointed again. It would have been a fairy-tale ending to a perfect season. Not perfect statistically but poetically. The Leafs had been mediocre through most of the regular season, but then they had gelled at just the right time and had managed to squeak into the play-offs.

They had won a tight series with the Florida Panthers. They had upset the New York Rangers and the Detroit Red Wings, two enormously talented and grossly overpaid teams. They'd kept winning because they weren't supposed to have been there in the first place. They'd played with reckless abandon against teams that had been heavily favored to swat them out of the way. They became a quintessential, Cinderella, upstart nuisance.

Because of the vagaries of the league's new wild card, crossover play-off system, they were up against their archrival, the Montreal Canadiens, the much-hated, evil incarnate—Lucifer himself on skates. It had seemed like fate. The only thing better than having broken a long Stanley Cup drought would have been breaking it at the expense of the spoiled child and teacher's pet of the NHL.

The world outside Toronto had moved on. Those things somehow happened. Gross negligence wasn't uncommon, and this would go down with the missed field goals, bobbled baseballs, and other historic catastrophes of sports lore.

Even in Toronto, the wounds were healing and the fans, toughened by decades of disappointment, were once again in that next-year frame of mind. Yuppie sports fans in the Center of the Known Universe turned their attention to other issues such as the Blue Jays' pitching problems, the Raptors' lack of a substantial backcourt, and the ongoing, never-ending effort of trying to get the National Football League's Bills to move north from Buffalo.

Ian, Zed, and Hunter were relaxing poolside on an early summer Saturday afternoon in Ian's parents' well-appointed backyard. Ian was drinking a rum and coke, Zed a beer, and Hunter his usual Red Bull and double vodka. Ian lay in the sun staring at the clouds while Zed and Hunter sat in the gazebo watching the Jays game on a portable TV.

Side by side, they were a study in physical contrast. For years, Hunter had overcompensated for the fact he was only five five and suffering from early onset male pattern baldness with obsessive bodybuilding and physical fitness. His shaved and tanned head sat atop a thick neck that sat upon more layers of muscles, a narrow waist, flat stomach, tree-trunk thighs, and calves that looked like frozen chickens. He accessorized his ridiculous anatomy with a diamond stud in one ear and a Leaf logo tattoo on his right bicep.

Zed was the opposite. He was six nine and skinny as a refugee. He wore his long, black hair in a ponytail and had a large, droopy mustache over what seemed to be a perpetual two-day beard. His only accessorizing was his ever-present, Easy Rider–style wraparound sunglasses.

Their personalities were polar opposites also. Hunter was the double espresso to Zed's decaf. He was easily agitated, had a short fuse, and was prepared to fight anyone, anywhere, and anytime over anything. Sometimes, if there was nothing to fight for, about, or over, he would pick a fight just for practice. And he'd usually win.

Zed on the other hand was probably the most laid-back person in the province. He was a quiet stoic with a world-class poker face but also a superb sense of humor. At first glance, one might think he was a stereotypical sixties hippie except for the fact that he couldn't be bothered to smoke dope and didn't have the ambition to protest anything. Tests confirmed that he was extremely intelligent, in the ninety-eighth percentile, and he had coasted through high school getting straight A's with very little effort. But his high IQ was counterbalanced by a very low MQ, his motivation quotient, as Ian called it. Rather than fully exploit his considerable intellect and pursue a career in academics or the sciences, he went directly from high school to the lifetime shelter and banal security of a job with Canada Post.

"I don't care what anyone says, the bastards stole it," Hunter said for approximately the nine-hundredth time. "Thieving bastards." Knowing his buddy had a unique skill for revenge, he turned to Zed. "Hey, how we gonna get back at them?"

Zed thought for a few seconds. He wholeheartedly agreed that the insult couldn't go unpunished, that the perpetrators had to understand there were consequences. "This calls for a public inquiry," he declared with his usual deadpan face. "A royal commission even. There should be hearings, reconciliation, compensation. The whole *kumbaya*. Our human rights have been violated."

"Let's make up one of those effigy dolls and go to Montreal and burn it!" Hunter suggested.

"Okay, we'll get in the Sex Box, drive to Montreal, and then burn a Flame doll outside the rink," said Ian.

The Sex Box was Zed's van. It was his baby, an eighties, vintage, full-sized, customized beauty that despite its age was kept in immaculate condition. It featured four plush, leather captain's chairs, an obscenely loud stereo, a fridge, a flat-screen TV, and a compact satellite dish that could be deployed on the roof. It served as an excellent mobile command center for parties, tailgating, and road trips. Naturally. it was painted Leaf blue.

"Then we can do the bars, hit a few strip clubs, a thing 'a beauty," Hunter added.

"Sounds great. We'll spend the night, have a late brunch, do a little shopping, and head home," Zed said. "Make a nice getaway weekend of it. I wonder if the Super 8 has a spa."

"Set flame to LaFlamme? I love it!" Ian said. "But you want to do it where people will see it, where it'll have impact, where they'll get the message. You want to make the TV news. There's city hall, but no one will be there on a weekend. There's Old Montreal, and they have a huge convention center and casino ..."

Schemes of protest, reprisal, and public spectacle began to fill their liquored imaginations.

"How about Notre Dame Cathedral?" Zed suggested. "It's probably the most visible landmark downtown. Imagine the chaos."

"The frogs are real touchy," Hunter said. "If we do this right, we can turn it into a type of national-unity thing. It'll be easy to get them to overreact and get all twisted up about this being some type of insult to their whole special-status, oppressed-minority, goddamn culture."

"If it's a slow day for news, the politicians can really sink their teeth into it," said Ian. "They all love this type of crap. Maybe get the PM involved." He saw visions of newspaper editorials, news conferences, and puffed-up declarations in the provincial legislature and House of Commons. Talking heads on television, endless pundits reflecting on the grave implications for the Dominion.

"Declarations will have to be declared! Offenses will have to be affronted! Grievances will have to be grieved. Civil disobedience is the arbiter of true justice," stated Zed, not sure if he was inadvertently quoting someone or if it had been an original thought. But damn, it sounded impressive.

"Then we'll find out where the Flame lives and spray-paint a big Leaf on his house just to top things off," Hunter said. "It'll be a thing 'a beauty."

"Can't hit the Flame's place. He's got only a condo there. In the off-season, he lives at his place on Georgian Bay," Ian said, recalling that factoid from an old profile in the *Hockey News*. "Huge place too, apparently."

"I'll bet he spends most of the summer catching up with Suzy," Hunter said. Suzy Sutton was a *Sports Illustrated* swimsuit model, an A-list celebrity, and LaFlamme's current girlfriend. But she was more than a mere supermodel. She was a goddess among goddesses. A physical specimen so perfect as to have no noticeable room for improvement. Every millimeter of her body, every line of her form, every tone of her color was perfect. It was as it Hugh Hefner had photoshopped his perfect woman and ordered her directly from God.

"I'd sure like to put my stick in her crease," said Hunter.

"Do you think she ever pulls his goalie?" Ian asked.

"LaFlamme likes playing with an extra man," Zed replied. "Besides, I think he probably pulls his own goalie."

"I'll bet she's a pretty good stick handler as well," Hunter said.

Double entendres about quick shifts, shin pads and the five hole continued for several minutes before they got back on topic.

"Okay, here it is," Hunter said. "We sneak up to his place on the lake, at night, like navy SEALS. We paint a big, blue Leaf on his deck. We piss in his pool, burn the doll, and haul ass outta there."

Stealing into a lakeside complex at night like a navy SEAL had an almost orgasmic appeal to Hunter and would fulfill one of his biggest fantasies. The only thing he had ever wanted in life was a career as a commando, military operative, mercenary, or undercover policeman—in that order. He had been rejected by the Canadian Armed Forces because his psychological profile was, to put it mildly, over the top. He'd been turned down by the Toronto police department for the same reason, but they had taken the easy way out and simply told him he was too short. He even had considerable difficulty getting his current job as a security guard at a vinegar factory. The only qualification most guards needed was to look a little imposing in a uniform. Unfortunately, the long-sleeved shirt, tight collar, tie, and military-style peaked cap hid his formidable physical assets. Rather than the well-muscled, finely tuned physical specimen he was, he simply looked like an angry little pug with high blood pressure. And why the hell did a vinegar factory need a security guard anyway?

A few minutes passed in silence.

"Gentlemen, I have the solution," said Ian, still lying on his back and staring at the clouds. "We, my fine, fine friends—" He sat up, removed his sunglasses for dramatic effect, and stared them in the eye. "—are going to steal the Stanley Cup."

The Stanley Cup is the most-storied trophy in major professional sports. It's also considered Canada's most valued treasure despite the fact it spends most of its time in the trophy cases of teams south of the border. Unlike the championship trophies for most other professional sports, it is a unique piece of hardware; there is only one Stanley Cup. The trophies for Major League Baseball, the NFL, and the NBA are simply copies reproduced every year and given to the winning teams to keep forever. The cup, on the other hand, has a history, a distinct bearing of majesty. It is a celebrity in its own right. It has toured the world several times, has been to the White House and the Kremlin and has done both Leno and Letterman. Babies have been baptized from it, and boatloads of champagne have been drunk from it.

It had been donated by the Englishman Lord Stanley, Earl of Preston and then governor general of Canada, in 1892. Despite having donated it, the good earl never got around to actually seeing a hockey game. Having paid his dues in the colonies, he hightailed it back to mother England at the first opportunity.

Sixteen teams had been victorious since the Leafs had last won. Most of them hadn't even existed in 1967, but of those, several had won the cup multiple times. This included teams in the dubious hockey markets of Dallas, Tampa Bay, Anaheim, and Raleigh, North Carolina of all places. But the most shameful statistic was the score of modern-day cup victories: Montreal 11–Toronto 1. A shameful ass kicking any way you measure it.

There is one other tradition about the Stanley Cup that's unique.

"Every player gets the cup for a full day after they win," said Ian.

"Yeah? So what?" asked Hunter.

"It's part of the deal. Everyone on the winning team, pine riders included, get it for twenty-four hours. They show it off at parades, take it to sick kiddies in the hospital, you know, that kind of feel-good, photo-op crap."

"So you want to hijack a parade and steal it," Zed said. "Didn't they do that in *Animal House*?"

"Not necessarily," said Ian. "Most of them make a big, showy deal of it, but some keep it low-key. They'll have their buddies over and eat nachos out of it, that sort of thing. We'll find out when one of these lazy buggers has it and steal it from him."

Zed and Hunter started to think it was more than a lazy, rum-fueled daydream. Their friend might actually be serious.

"Okay," Zed said sarcastically, "we break into someone's house and steal the cup from some six-four, two-hundred-pound defenseman and his drunken cronies during movie night. That plan needs some work. We need to hammer out a few details. Let me think about it and get back to you."

Ian started pacing beside the pool as ideas quickly began forming in his head. "Not necessarily. There's twenty-five guys on the roster, and they each get it for one day, plus there's travel time. It's gonna have to go everywhere from Stockholm, Sweden to Rat's Ass, Saskatchewan, and everywhere else in between. Somewhere in there, we'll get our chance. We just have to look for it."

He began building steam. He genuinely wanted to sell the idea to his friends. "Let's just do it. I'm serious, guys. For once in our sorry little lives, let's get off our asses and do something important." He sounded like a high-priced lawyer making an emotional summation to a skeptical jury. "They stole it from us. We're going to steal it back. It's as simple as that."

"Sounds like a plan," Hunter said, never being one to waste time considering the long-term consequences of his actions. "Sign me up."

"You're nuts! You realize if we get caught, we'll do hard time," said Zed after having mulled it over for a few seconds.

"Then let's not get caught," Ian said. "But even if we do, we'll be folk heroes! We'll get a slap on the wrist, do six months in minimum security, and sell the movie rights."

There was a long pause.

"Well … chicks do dig rebels," Zed pointed out.

"Thing 'a beauty," responded Hunter, his eyes showing he was getting pumped about the idea.

"Sounds good. I'm in," said Zed after thinking about it a few more seconds. He slumped back in his lounger, pulled his sunglasses down from his forehead, and pointed his face to the sun. "It'll make the news, I guarantee that."

Chapter 4
Vengeance Is a Dish Best Served Frozen

Despite what they said at the time, none of them was a hundred percent sure about the caper. It had sounded like a neat idea at the time, but after the liquor had worn off, they knew they still weren't actually committed to it.

Even so, with a long summer ahead of them and precious little else to do, they started to casually hammer out the details at their regular poolside meetings. If nothing else, it would be an entertaining and somewhat inebriated intellectual exercise.

Ian, the architect of the operation, took charge of the logistics and planning. Zed concentrated on intelligence— finding out the details, the whos, whats, wheres, and whatnots. Hunter eagerly used the opportunity to exercise his paramilitary fantasies and began researching equipment and matériel. He also insisted that like any great military mission it be given a name. They considered Lord Stanley's Liberation, Revenge of the Leafs, Covert Cup Rescue, and others. After kicking it around for a few days, they came to an agreement and christened it Operation Silver Justice.

Over the summer, the cup would make its rounds to the homes of all the Canadiens' players. Zed determined that it would be doing a circuit though several spots in Canada, a few in the States, two in Scandinavia, and one in eastern Europe.

Logistics, legal considerations, and their budget or lack thereof dictated that they would have to liberate the cup during one of its Canadian stops. Zed managed to get the itinerary with unexpected ease. A few emails to the league under the guise of a fan who wanted his picture taken with the cup yielded an accurate list of who would have it when and where.

Further investigation of fan websites and blogs gave them a fairly accurate indication of what sort of activity each player had planned for his time with the cup. Small-town heroes would take it to their local fairs and show it along with the prize-winning heifers and rhubarb pies. In bigger centers, they would take it to children's hospitals, old folks' homes, and the like. It would also doubtlessly make many unscheduled stops at bars, beach parties, and softball tournaments.

One by one, they went through the list, narrowing it down. In the end, they came up with four possibilities all within driving distance of Toronto and in small centers or less-populated areas. One spot in particular proved intriguing.

"It meets all our criteria," said Zed.

They had gone as far as setting up a little war room in the Andrews's game room. He pointed to a large map of Ontario laid out on the pool table. "It's only a few hours' drive, it's accessible by water, and it has lots of surrounding forest cover. It'll keep the travel expenses down, and there are no borders to cross. In my opinion, it's the only logical option."

"Logical and yet so poetic," Ian said. "I can't think of a more fitting target."

"Me neither," Hunter said. "Can we hit it tomorrow?"

In the following days, they walked through their plan several more times, drawing out a flowchart on a whiteboard and trying to anticipate problems and plan contingencies. Everything seemed to fit. Hunter assured them that he could beg, borrow, steal, buy, or rent all the necessary equipment.

"If you believe in this type of thing," said Ian, "and I don't, but if you did, this opportunity is so, so ...

serendipitous as to seem to be nothing short of divine intervention." The sheer karma suddenly and manifestly changed the plan from a fun fantasy exercise to a reality they wholeheartedly and unquestioningly committed themselves to. They considered it a celestial decree from the stars in the heavens. The gods of hockey had come down to their end of the bench, tapped them on the shoulder, and told them to get out there and get the job done. They were the chosen enforcers charged with retaliating for the insult of the previous game.

The same providence that opened this window of opportunity also made it perfectly clear that it would be slammed shut in less than three weeks. Executing their plan suddenly took on an urgency that consumed their every free hour. They worked long hours with a high level of focus and determination, a new and unusual experience for each of them. Locations had to be scouted, arrangements had to be made, and equipment had to be secured. On schedule and with surprisingly few complications, everything seemed to fall in place.

"I feel it's my job to reiterate one important point," Ian pronounced to the other two as they were wrapping up their last planning session. "In the cold, cold light of day, this is a premeditated and fairly serious crime. This isn't simply an adolescent prank. It's not the type of thing the police will give us a night in jail and a slap on the wrist for just to scare us. It's only a few degrees this side of armed robbery. If we get caught, we'll without a doubt spend some time as guests of Her Majesty. It's essential that we're all clear that—"

"We're all clear and we all don't care," Hunter interrupted Ian's little speech. "Operation Silver Justice is officially green lighted. It's a thing 'a beauty."

"Agreed. It's lit, it's green, and it's good to go," said Zed.

Good to go, Ian thought. He imagined his father encouraging him: "That's my boy. Put all those 'ologies to good use and go out and steal a hockey trophy."

At midmorning on a pleasant Saturday in late August, they rolled the Sex Box up to Paddleman's Marina on Georgian Bay. They had reserved a water-ski boat for twenty-four hours ostensibly to do a bit of skiing, some touring, and overnight camping. They filled it with skis, coolers, and various other pieces of equipment and roared out onto the lake. After a little water skiing, they spent a few hours cruising the shoreline, gawking at the multimillion-dollar, lakeside palaces, and trolling for young rich things in bikinis.

Late in the afternoon, they pulled onto a small spit of an island and settled in for what would appear to other boaters as a drunken, late-afternoon picnic. Most islands on the lake were dotted with moderate-sized cottages, and those that weren't usually had squatters partying on them. Their tiny island had no redeeming features and rarely attracted any visitors. The island they had chosen was too narrow to build on; it was surrounded by rocks that made landing a boat a bit of a challenge, and the only vegetation was a few spindly pine trees and very thick brush. Geographically, however, it was strategically invaluable; it was a mere hundred yards from the ostentatious waterfront chateau of the hero of that year's Stanley Cup final and the target of their operation, Laurent LaFlamme.

The Flame's sprawling, multilevel affair had a series of terraced decks descending from the main house to the waterfront. The large deck near the house had a pool, a bar, and a fully equipped outdoor kitchen. The pool featured a waterfall that emptied into a larger pool on the deck below, bracketed by two waterslides. Various elaborate gazebos, stone fireplaces, and hot tubs filled in the smaller decks toward the shore.

A boathouse bigger than a typical Mississauga split-level housed a 300-hp, twin-engine jet speedboat, a classic, wooden Chris Craft, a large party barge, jet skis, canoes, kayaks, and miscellaneous other watercraft. The guys wouldn't have been surprised to see a small submarine moored there as well. The only thing missing was a helicopter pad.

The design of the compound had a contemporary feel while still complementing its magnificent natural setting. It featured acres of glass, natural stone, and exposed timbers all capped by an almost-flat roof angled elegantly toward the water. Various trees, shrubs, and planters full of immaculate flowers punctuated the property. Dense groves of trees bordered both sides, giving it full privacy from the neighboring estates. It was the type of place Frank Lloyd Wright would have designed for James Bond as a weekend retreat.

As soon as the sun went down, they moved to the leeward side of their tiny island base and started to set up their equipment. After changing into an assortment of camouflage clothing, they pulled together a crude blind of reeds and branches. Hunter mounted large, extremely powerful binoculars on a sturdy tripod. Next to that was another tripod holding a parabolic microphone, and a third had a sophisticated digital camera with a very long telephoto lens. Ian set up a radio scanner that would allow him to listen to any police communication, security personnel's walkie-talkies, and various other sundry radio traffic. They settled in for a long wait.

Zed's diligent intelligence work had determined that LaFlamme didn't plan to make a big fuss of his day with the cup. When he had pretended to be a rabid fan and called the public relations office of the Canadiens about getting his photo taken with the trophy and his "hero," LaFlamme, they had referred him to LaFlamme's agent, who bounced the request on to another flunky. They had apologetically told him that LaFlamme had planned a private function at his home that day and wasn't going to make any public appearances with the cup. She had offered to send him an autographed picture as a consolation. Zed had gushed his thanks over the phone, gave her a phony name and address, and hung up.

Further investigation confirmed that it was indeed going to be held at his castle on the lake. He'd already won the cup twice on his previous stint with the Red Wings, so it wasn't as big a deal as it was for first-time winners. His plan was to have a small gathering of his teammates, a few of his and Suzy's celebrity friends, and their least-unattractive relatives.

They dug in and watched as the party unfolded over the next few hours. LaFlamme and Suzy mingled with the guests while attractive young girls in shorts and tank tops circulated with drinks and appetizers. The guests were was a disappointing mixture of nobodies, other hockey players, and at best C-list celebrities. It was strictly Canadian content with the exception of one guy Zed thought might be one of the Foo Fighters.

The cup was front and center on a small, draped pedestal beside the waterfall. Some dimwit had decided that the most historic trophy in the world would be filled not with champagne or caviar or dozens of red roses but a variety of Pepsi products carefully arranged on a bed of crushed ice garnished with lemons, limes, and cherries. There were bottles of Diet Pepsi, Caffeine-Free Diet, High-Caffeine Diet, Lemon, Lime, Cherry, and regular Pepsi. Pepsi was one of LaFlamme's biggest endorsement contracts, and Ian was certain there was a significant fee involved in this vulgar layout. From time to time, guests would help themselves to a bottle, and in less than a minute, it would be replaced with an identical bottle in the same spot.

Much to their surprise, the party started winding down around midnight, early by celebrity standards. By one in the morning, all the guests and the catering staff were gone. LaFlamme and Suzy lingered on the unlit deck but still in full view of the island. On top of everything else, the gods of hockey had blessed them with a clear evening and a full moon—perfect conditions for the sophisticated night-vision equipment Hunter had procured.

After a few minutes, LaFlamme and Suzy wandered hand in hand to the pedestal where the cup sat. He wiped the inside dry with some paper towels, dipped his fingers

41

into Suzy's bikini top, and pulled out a small plastic envelope. He opened it, turned, and tap-tap-tapped some fine white powder into the cup.

"This is interesting," Ian said from behind the binoculars. "They're doing coke. They're actually snorting cocaine from the Stanley Cup." He restrained himself from making the obvious joke about the trophy being filled with coke and Pepsi on the same evening.

"You're right. That is interesting," Zed said. "We should get pictures."

"I'm already on it," said Hunter as he snapped away with the camera.

"I'm sure the league would be quite concerned if they knew one of their stars was a cokehead," said Ian sarcastically. "It's my understanding that this type of thing is frowned upon."

"No, I don't think the league would be concerned at all if they knew one of their stars was a cokehead," Zed said. "I think they would, however, be quite concerned if they knew *we* knew one of their stars was a cokehead."

LaFlamme and Suzy had gone down to the large, stone hot tub on one of the lower decks. They stripped naked. For a few precious moments, the coke-snorting, cup-stealing, offside-skating hockey star stood beside the fabulous, swimsuit-modeling, *People*-magazine, top-ten sexy celebrity, and gloriously, nakedly, stunningly awesome Suzy Sutton. Talk about a thing 'a beauty. He held her hand as she stepped into the bubbling water and slid in after her. The entire magnificent spectacle had lasted only a few seconds. In the blink of an eye, it was over.

But they had pictures. Lots of pictures.

Operation Silver Justice was a go.

Chapter 5
Operation Silver Justice

With Zed providing reconnaissance from the command post in the bush, Ian and Hunter started out. Rather than go straight across the short stretch of water, Hunter decided to circle around from the far side of the island, cross over a few hundred yards down from LaFlamme's, and approach his dock along the shore. He had hoped to secure a navy-SEAL, special-ops quality, self-inflating launch craft with a super-silent electric motor, but their budget simply hadn't allowed that. Instead, they had to make do with a plastic novelty from Canadian Tire that they had spray-painted matte black to cover up its original lime-green color and alligator appliqués. It came with two pairs of matching water wings that Ian had given serious thought to bringing along, just in case.

During the planning phase, they'd had a small dispute over who would do what on the mission. All three wanted to be in on the assault, and there was no way Hunter wasn't going to be one of them. But there was room for only two in their craft, and Ian finally convinced Zed that getting his lanky frame into what was essentially a toy raft was analogous to packing a fishing rod into a glove compartment.

As they paddled, Ian cursed himself for not being in better physical condition. Fortunately, they had been able to talk Hunter out of his original plan to swim across underwater with scuba gear.

They pulled in under the large dock and moored the raft to a post. Hunter hopped onto the deck in a one-piece, black, neoprene wetsuit with matching booties and a diver's bonnet. He had disguised his face with black greasepaint. He rounded out the outfit with a diver's watch, a large knife on his belt, and a monocular night-vision device strapped to his forehead. The ensemble was impressive. He didn't look like the kind of person anyone would consider messing with.

Ian struggled a little harder to pull himself onto the dock; he just barely escaped falling into the water. He wore an all-black ensemble of sweatpants, a long-sleeved

T-shirt, chunky hiking boots, and a woolen ski mask. His entire kit, which had cost him $5 at the Salvation Army, was already soaked in sweat from the trip over.

Both wore small headsets attached to walkie-talkies on their belts.

"Landed. Awaiting orders," Hunter whispered into his radio.

"They're still in the hot tub," Zed said. "The puppy is another level up on the bench." *Puppy* was the code word they'd given the cup. They had worked through a number of different scenarios, knowing they would have to make fast battlefield decisions as circumstances demanded. It had to be some form of a snatch-and-grab because as zealous as they were, they weren't prepared to hold the Flame and Suzy up with a weapon or engage in any type of standoff. They had figured that would turn their caper from a minor to a major crime and exponentially increase their jail time should they get caught.

Because of the terraced layout of the property, Zed could see and hear almost everything with his surveillance gear from the island. He was their eyes and ears and entrusted with command of that phase of the operation. They all knew the who, what, where, and why of the mission. The how was going to be the tricky part, and they knew right from the outset they'd have to make that part up on the fly. Zed would direct them step by step, and it was agreed by all that he would have the final say, including if necessary the option to abort the mission.

"As it stands now, you'd have to run up three decks to get it and then back," Zed told them. "I don't see any way there that doesn't pass by the tub."

"How about through the grove of trees to the right?" asked Ian.

"Negative," Zed responded. "It's pretty thick growth. You'd have to use your lights and also hack through it. It would make a bunch of noise."

"Screw it," said Hunter. "I say we just run for it. By the time that prick gets out of the tub, we'll be gone."

"Negative again," Zed replied. "Much as I respect your manhood, I don't want to put you up against a coked-up hockey player defending his chick. I also don't want to risk a bunch of noise. Sound carries a long way on the water, and we mustn't alert the neighbors. Hold your positions for now. I don't think they're going to be in there too long."

"Understood," Ian responded.

Successful operations required not only stealth and courage but great patience as well. This was one of the many points Hunter had stressed to them repeatedly in their pre-mission briefings. They also had the considerable advantages of the night and surprise on their side.

"What scenarios are we looking at here?" Ian asked after a few minutes of silence, thinking that they may as well try to anticipate the various situations while they were waiting. He also found it difficult to go long periods without talking.

"Best case, they pass out in the tub, we waltz in, grab the puppy, waltz out," said Zed.

"I still say I can take the prick while he's bobbing for Suzy's apples." Hunter said.

"Negative, Benji," Zed said firmly. "Not an option."

Benji was Hunter's code name in keeping with the canine theme. He would have preferred Bulldog, Pitbull, or Rin Tin Tin, but as is the case with most military nicknames, his had been given to him by his colleagues; he'd had no say in the matter. Ian had been dubbed Lassie, and Zed was Scooby-Doo. The model and the hockey player were Lady and the Tramp respectively, although Hunter would refer to the Tramp only as "that prick."

"Screw this. I'm gone," Hunter whispered to Ian without turning his microphone on. In a flash, he leaped to the next level, scampered the entire length of the deck, and crouched behind a stone fireplace. The same man who had preached the importance of patience and stealth suddenly had his attention deficit disorder flare up and had gone rogue.

"Scooby, Benji has taken off," Ian whispered over the radio to Zed.

"Benji, stay," Zed commanded, not realizing the irony of the command.

"Benji ten-seven," replied Hunter, indicating by universal radio code that he was turning his radio off and would be incommunicado.

"What the hell's he doing?" Ian asked, unable to see anything from his position.

"Dumb bastard. It looks like he's going to try to find his own way up to the house," said Zed while zooming in on him through the binoculars.

"If he screws this up, I'll kill the asshole," Ian said.

"Lassie, you have my clearance to do so," said Zed.

Over the next ten minutes, Hunter silently and skillfully zigzagged his way up to the house. Zed described his moves in detail to Ian, stranded on the bottom deck. Using surprisingly catlike maneuvers, Hunter swung himself onto the next-higher deck and rolled to the far edge, keeping out of the line of sight of the hot tub. He crawled on his elbows to the far end to the same thick grove of overgrown spruce Zed had earlier ruled out as an access route.

Rather than hacking his way through the trees, he took advantage of the various well-kept shrubs planted alongside. He crouched behind the first bush. He slowly rose to check on the tub with the cyclops-like night-vision scope strapped to his black-hooded head. With LaFlamme and the girl paying no attention to anything but each other, he leapfrogged to the next bush and rose slowly to scope them out. He repeated this procedure a half-dozen times until he was beside the house.

Zed could see him crouched below the main patio a mere twenty feet from the large, glass sliding door. He held his breath and was furiously trying to send him telepathic messages to not go any closer to the door. It was in clear view of the hot tub and most certainly had a motion sensor that would flood the area with light if activated.

Throughout this whole event, Ian sat fuming on the dock listening to Zed's play-by-play through his earpiece. He was furious with Hunter, but at the same time, he kept his fingers crossed that he would pull it off nonetheless. The benevolent hands of the gods of hockey would surely guide and protect him on his courageous quest.

Zed's telepathy must have gotten through; rather than making a dash for the door, Hunter executed two summersaults back through the shrubs and disappeared beside the house. Not only did they have no radio contact with him, they had no visual contact either. Zed had no clue of what Hunter would be up against. Despite all their reconnaissance work, it had never occurred to them to simply drive by the front of the house just to see what might be there. For all he knew, there could be anything from rabid guard dogs or moats filled with alligators to automatic machine-gun turrets. Hunter had embarked on a covert black op of his own design. The fate of the entire mission was now in his tiny, but muscular hands.

After helplessly marinating in his own sweat in a dark corner of the dock for nearly half an hour, Ian started to panic. "This is *not* going well," he radioed Zed. "I don't like the way this is going. I think we need to pull out and cut our losses. I think we need to abort."

"Negative, Lassie," Zed responded coolly. "Nothing's happening yet, and we agreed that was strictly my call. Besides, you know my position on abortion."

Zed's joke and confident demeanor helped relax Ian.

"Hang on ... the bastard's on the roof!"

Slowly, dramatically, Hunter's black silhouette emerged on the flat roof of the large house. He walked carefully toward the front edge and paused for a moment. With the full August moon behind him and scattered clouds framing his profile, he was indeed an impressive sight. His arms hung at his side, spread ever so slightly. His weight was on one leg; the other was bent at the knee and cocked for action. Zed was certain that he had practiced that very pose hundreds of times in front of the mirror. If Hunter had had a cape and small pointy ears, Zed would have sworn he was looking at Batman.

Hunter got down on all fours and slowly crept to the edge. He reached down, grabbed the gutter, executed a reverse-flip, midair summersault, and made a perfect, silent gymnastic, two-point landing on the balcony. "Superb," Zed whispered. "Ten points from the Russian judge." He saw the glass door slide open a few feet and quickly close.

He had done it. The little bugger had done it. He's a hero, tonight's first star, *la premiere etoile*. The security guard from the vinegar factory has successfully and single-handedly penetrated the multimillion-dollar fortress of a major sports celebrity. He's much more than a special-op commando. He's now a true, certified, macho-stud Ninja.

"Benji ten eight," Hunter said through the radio to indicate he was back in communication. "I'm in the house."

"I see that." Zed was relieved. "Good work, but you're still an asshole."

"Your mother and I were worried sick," Ian added, trying to sound calm. "Next time, call us and let us know where you are."

"You can dock my pay," he replied. "What do we do from here?"

Zed had formulated a plan while watching Hunter's assault on the house. "Go to the main floor. Find a spot where you can hide but still see the back door. It's just a matter of time before they head to the house. We don't want to ambush them as soon as they come in. I want them well inside the house, in their bedroom or something, so that any screaming and yelling won't be heard outside."

"Ten four," Hunter responded.

"Lassie, hold your position," Zed said. "When they start heading up to the house, you follow. When you're at the door, Benji will give you click codes when it's okay to go inside."

Earlier, Hunter had taught them a simple code that allowed them to communicate by clicking the call button on the walkie-talkie when it wasn't safe to talk. "Check-a-roo, Scooby Doo," Ian responded.

"Ten four. Scooby-Doo to you, soldier," Zed replied.

Within a few minutes, Lady and the Tramp started to stir. They got out of the hot tub, put on thick, terrycloth robes, and climbed the stairs to the main patio. LaFlamme held her hand as she wobbled her way up, clearly showing the effects of the evening's intoxicants.

When they got to the house, the bright floodlights turned on automatically, confirming Zed's guess about there being a motion detector. LaFlamme went to the fridge in the outdoor bar and grabbed a bottle of wine. He put his other arm around the Stanley Cup and motioned in a gentlemanly fashion for Suzy to go inside.

"Lassie, you're clear to proceed to the back door but stay out of the light," said Zed. "Benji, you'd better be well hidden 'cause they're in the house."

Hunter responded by clicking the code that everything was okay.

Ian ascended to the top patio, stopping several times to catch his breath. He wasn't as well prepared for the long series of stairs as he should have been. The difficulty of climbing in heavy boots, soggy sweatpants, and a ski mask on a warm, August evening was something he realized he could have better thought through.

"Benji, Lassie's at the back door," Zed said, again not realizing the pun. "Is it safe for him to go in?"

Hunter clicked yes. Ian crawled into the large kitchen.

"Okay, boys Remember 'Pinball Wizard? Well you can call me Tommy now 'cause I'm the deaf, dumb, and blind kid," Zed said. "You're on your own from here. Let me know how things turn out. And try not to get killed. I don't know how I'd explain any of this to your parents."

Chapter 6
The Neutral-Zone Trap

The interior of LaFlamme's lakeshore mansion was every bit as grand and over the top as was the exterior. The entire main floor was an enormous, multilevel great room the size of a high school gym with the same wood, glass, and stone motif as the exterior. Along one side was a dining area with a table large enough to easily seat an entire hockey team including coaches, trainers, and stick boy. On the opposite side was a mini nightclub area including a long glass bar with about a thousand liquor bottles arranged on a backlit wall. There was a six-by-twelve-foot snooker table, a poker table, a variety of pinball machines, and a small dance floor. An anteroom had a leather-walled home theater area that could be shut off from the rest of the room with sliding wooden panels. A closet-sized humidor and climate-controlled wine room rounded out the space.

The focal point of the room was a massive, walk-in stone fireplace large enough to roast a small calf on a spit. It was circled by two massive leather sofas and matching easy chairs. Directly in front of the fireplace was a genuine, pure-white, twelve-foot-long polar bear rug complete with tail, claws, and head.

A broad, semicircular, solid-oak staircase led to the second floor, where Hunter waited, crouched behind a large banister. "Lassie, I'm in the big room on the stairs," Hunter whispered in the walkie-talkie. "Wait till you see the size of this room. Stay put until I figure out where they're going, got it?"

Ian clicked the code for message understood.

Lady and the Tramp, with the puppy in tow, continued into the great room. He set the cup on the hearth and lit the kindling under the huge logs that had been laid out. Suzy let her robe fall to the floor. She warmed her naked body while the fire roared to life. She stretched out on the bearskin rug as if posing for a photo shoot. LaFlamme took another small packet of white powder from his robe pocket, tapped some cocaine onto the glass-topped coffee table, and started to divide it into lines.

He gave a straw to Suzy, and just as she sat up to take a snort, a round, black figure popped up from behind the adjacent sofa.

"Say cheese!" Hunter yelled.

They turned to face him just in time to be hit with the bright flash from his small digital camera.

"Come on in, Lassie. We're by the fire," he shouted toward the kitchen while taking more pics.

The hockey player and the supermodel froze. They were speechless. They rubbed and blinked their eyes from the blinding flash.

"Sorry to alarm you," Ian said as nonchalantly as he could as he walked into the room. "We just need a little extra insurance." He tried to project an air of calm and sophistication, but his heart was beating so hard he could barely keep his knees from buckling as sat down beside them on one of the large chairs.

It hit him like a bucket of ice water and he nearly fainted. He was actually sitting in Larry the Flame's living room. The Stanley Cup itself, the real deal, was waiting for them to take it. Suzy Sutton, arguably the most beautiful woman in the world, was sitting nude, shamelessly flaunting her naughty bits on the floor not five feet away. And Ian was in charge! For a few seconds, his entire nervous system almost short-circuited and seized up. He leaned back in the chair, tried to pull himself together, took a deep breath, and spoke.

"Please relax. We promise we're not here to hurt you." That came out a lot weaker than he had hoped. His voice had almost cracked. He quietly cleared his throat. "Just a little unfinished business. We need to right some wrongs."

Suzy finally came to her senses and scrambled for her robe. That was a good thing. It made it easier for Ian to concentrate and put his fishing rod back into his glove compartment.

"What the hell?" were the only words LaFlamme could quietly squeak out. He gathered his thoughts as quickly as he could under the circumstances. He determined that all things considered, it was best not to resist. His whole career could be vaporized by the pictures inside the stubby frogman's camera. He also had no idea of how many there were of the intruders or if they were armed to say nothing of the fact that he was stoned and wearing nothing but a short bathrobe that didn't go down even as far as his knees.

There was only a tiny yelp from Suzy, likely because she was heavily anesthetized from the effects of the booze and drugs on her hundred-and-five-pound body. She darted over to the couch beside LaFlamme and just sat there with a slack-jawed, glazed stare, looking as if she might have just peed herself, which she had probably done.

Ian was a little more comfortable immersing himself in the role of the gentleman thief behind the safety of his ski mask. He sat back in the overstuffed chair, crossed his legs, and went as far as to tent his rubber-gloved fingers as he spoke. He continued as casually as he could. He explained to the pair frozen on the couch who they were and why they were there. Hunter stood at his side like a henchman, still shooting pictures every few seconds.

It was nothing personal, he explained. It was just that LaFlamme had made a mistake and, admittedly through no fault of his own, it had resulted in the Stanley Cup being mistakenly awarded to the wrong team. It really was the referee's fault, and though Ian and his friends were understandably upset with LaFlamme, they really held no animosity for him personally. It was important that he understood that.

That last part was a lie. They hated the Hab bastard with every fiber of their being.

As he continued his fireside chat, he noticed out of the corner of his eye that Hunter's attention deficit disorder had flared up again. The wet-suited wonder was wandering around the great room with his camera, shooting pictures of everything and anything as if he were at a museum taking snapshots of old dinosaur bones. The next thing, Ian thought, was that Hunter was going to ask if it would be okay to take a quick tour of the bedrooms and en-suites upstairs. He gave him a firm glance over his shoulder that said, *Knock it off you idiot and get the hell over here this instant!*

"You should also know that if you're even thinking of overpowering us, another of our colleague has several other pictures of you in the hot tub outside. Naughty stuff that." He winked at Suzy, whose perfect, china-doll complexion turned an even paler shade of white. "Anyhow, we don't need to inconvenience you any further. We'll just take the trophy and go," he said as he stood. "Can you tell me where the case is?"

LaFlamme gestured toward the bar, and Hunter sauntered over there to retrieve the cup's sarcophagus.

"You guys are morons, you know," LaFlamme said as his nerve began to return. "You're gonna get caught."

"You're may be right, indeed, but such are the risks we take in life." He started laying it on thick. His speech and mannerisms had become a syrupy mélange of every detective and spy movie he had ever seen that even Hunter was rolling his eyes. "What must be done must be done. Now, we're going to impose on you for one last thing," Ian said politely. "Just to make everything official. My friend's camera can also take short video clips. I'm going to ask you to stand beside the trophy and read what's on this card while he records it."

LaFlamme was indignant, but he knew he had no option but to cooperate. He got up from the sofa, plucked the card from Ian's hand, stood beside the cup, and started to read aloud the card's message.

"I'm Laurent LaFlamme of the Montreal Canadiens. I make this statement of my own free will." He spoke haltingly with a mild Québécois accent as he read. "In this year's Stanley Cup, I was clearly offside before I scored the goal that won the final game. Therefore, it should not have counted. This trophy—" He awkwardly turned and pointed to it as though it were a prize on a game show. "—rightly belongs to the Toronto Maple Leafs, and I hereby call upon league officials to exercise their right to overturn the results and award it to them. The people doing this are good, decent, and honest men who promise to return the cup to the league promptly and unharmed after that's done. Thank you."

"That's great, just great," Ian said. "And you did it on the first take. Excellent."

"Hang on," Hunter said. "Make him do it again for the frogs."

"Good thinking, Benji," Ian replied in a somewhat patronizing voice. "And very culturally sensitive I

63

might add. How about one more take *en français* for your
countrymen? I'll let you translate it on your own."

LaFlamme frowned, looked at the card, and began
speaking again, "Je suis Laurent LaFlamme sur la
Montreal Canadiens …"

When he finished, Ian rolled the heavy case to the
fireplace while Hunter stood guard with the prisoners
on the couch. He carefully pulled the heavy velvet bag
over the trophy, placed it in the sturdy, black case, and
latched it all up.

"Okay. That's all we need. Rest assured we'll take
good care of this treasure. We are not in this for any
money, and it will eventually make it back to where it
rightfully belongs intact. I promise you that." Ian said.
"Now here's the plan. Please don't call anyone until the
morning. You went to bed, having left the cup locked
up in your kitchen, and when you woke up, it was gone.
Okay? That's your story, simple as that."

Unprovoked, Suzy let out another quiet yelp as her
tiny mind tried to process everything going on. Her face
had turned even paler, almost to the point of transparency.

"We really do appreciate your continued cooperation,
and you have my word we will not resort to using our
insurance unless absolutely necessary. It's been an honor
meeting you sir. Ms. Sutton, a pleasure as well." He turned
and gave her a half-bow. "Enjoy the rest of your evening."

They exited, pulling the cup behind them.

"Scooby-Doo, this is Lassie. The puppy's on the leash."

In less than twenty minutes, they had paddled their vinyl alligator dingy back to the small island. Zed met them at the water's edge, where he safely got the cup transferred to the ski boat while Hunter deflated the raft. Ian focused his attention on kneeling in the shallow water and throwing up several times. "Cheer up, soldier," Zed said to him drolly while handing him a bottle of Gatorade. "There's probably a Purple Heart in this for you."

They packed up all their gear, picked up every molecule of debris, and removed any other trace of their presence as per Hunter's detailed instructions. They straightened any broken or bent branches and raked the ground behind them as they walked toward the shore on the far side.

By dawn, they were in the Sex Box heading to Toronto. Zed was careful to set the van's cruise control at exactly five miles per hour over the speed limit. Naturally, he didn't want to be stopped for speeding, but he didn't want to go so slow and draw attention to himself for that reason. Nothing made the police more suspicious on Ontario highways than someone driving at or below the speed limit. It was a very reliable indicator that the driver was drinking, already drunk, smoking dope, or literally trying to stay below the radar.

The gods of hockey saluted the successfully completion of their assignment with a glorious purple sunrise over the millions of pines trees lining the road. Hunter was still on an adrenaline high; he was bobbing his head and lip-synching silently to some song playing in his head. Ian's respiration and heart rate had finally returned to normal, but his mind still raced, oscillating between disbelief that their plan had actually worked and worrying how things would inevitably go wrong.

Zed wore his Canada Post, standard-issue, blank, expressionless face as he drove. Ian had always admired Zed's stoicism; he could never tell what was going on in his mind. He would display the same persona regardless of whether he had just won the lottery or if his entire family had been murdered. It was such good emotional control that Ian wondered if it had been self-taught, neo-Zen behavior or some type of neurological defect.

There was no music or conversation. The only sound was the baritone hum of the van's acoustically tuned exhaust. They drove for several miles before Hunter broke the silence.

"So what do we do now?"

Chapter 7
Rebels without a Clue

"It has been confirmed, my friends. It was first announced late this morning by Roger McMillan, president of the National Hockey League, and later verified by the OPP and the RCMP—" Vaughn Tedesco of CTTR radio spoke in a slow yet excited voice. "—that the Stanley Cup has been stolen. According to the league announcement, the Stanley Cup was stolen sometime last night from the lakeside home of Laurent LaFlamme. It was the guest of honor, if you will, at a small gathering for family and friends. When he awoke earlier this morning, he discovered, much to his shock and surprise I'm sure, that his cottage had been broken into and the cup had been stolen.

"In a telephone call received by this station less than ten minutes ago, a group calling itself the LJS, the Leaf Justice Squad, called with their demands. Let's not dilly-dally any longer. We'll just go straight to that call now."

Listeners heard an electronically distorted voice. "We are the LJS, the Leaf Justice Squad. We have the Stanley Cup in our possession and will return it safely when and only after our demands have been met. We call on the board of governors of the National Hockey League to void the results of game seven of this year's Stanley Cup finals and declare the Toronto Maple Leafs the league's champions for this season. The awarding of the championship to the Montreal Canadiens was a travesty and the biggest outrage in the history of sport. This team was the victim of an obvious collusion between executives of the NHL, the referees, and the Francocentric political elite. This must not stand. We await your response." Click.

"Well, there you have it, my friends," Tedesco said. "This call has been traced, oddly enough, to a telephone booth at a shopping mall in Buffalo. In all honesty, I have to say that while I abhor their reprehensible tactics, I am in some strange way sympathetic to the sentiments of the so-called Leaf Justice Squad. And I suspect, my friends, that many of you may feel the same. It is indeed a moral dilemma. Is this another of those rare occasions in history when violation of the law is subordinate to a greater good, a grander purpose? Only time will tell. Let's open the phones."

The theft was front-page stuff throughout North America. Coming as it did, in the late summer when any interesting news was in very short supply, it was a godsend to the media. It was a near-perfect news story. A high-profile theft. A valuable treasure. Noble bandits with selfless ransom demands. Some saw it as grassroots hockey fans reclaiming the game from the circus promoters who were squeezing every dime they could out of it. It appealed to people's lurid fascination with crime but without the marketing drawbacks of gruesome murders, serial killings, or dead bodies. For the first time in years, the major media had a glossy, big-budget, blockbuster crime story. And best of all, it was rated G. It was a felony the whole family could enjoy.

The prime minister stood in the House to express his outrage and promised decisive action but without giving specifics. The premiers of Ontario and Quebec followed suit. Stern motions were made. Unanimous resolutions were passed. During the question period in the House, the leader of the opposition used all his histrionic skills to make the heist look like the fault of the governing party.

The public of course lapped it up. Every avenue of the internet was on fire. Sports shock jockeys could barely contain their glee as they yelled into their microphones.

Frustrated Leaf fans drove down the street honking horns, yelling out their windows, and flying makeshift banners, "Godspeed LJS!" and "LJS = Truth" among them. Stores sold T-shirts reading "Honorary member— LJS," "President LJS Fan Club," "Kiss me, I'm LJS," "Gandhi—Mandela— LJS." One creative vendor took the National Rifle Association's iconic poster of Charlton Heston holding a rifle in the air and superimposed a Leaf jersey on him. He was holding the cup above his head. The text on the poster wrote itself: "You can have this trophy when you pry it from my cold, dead hands."

The story played just as well on *Entertainment Tonight* as it did on *60 Minutes*. It made the front page of everything from the *Wall Street Journal* to the *National Enquirer* and everything in between. *As it Happens*, *W5*, *Larry King*, *Lloyd Robertson*, and even *Saturday Night Live* all harvested its rich content. Even in the tabloids, Kim Kardashian and Taylor Swift had been usurped by a hundred-year-old hockey trophy.

Toronto had always been a New York City wannabe, and its residents collectively reveled in the attention they were suddenly getting from the American media. Of course they wanted the cup to be found—but just not too soon. This story had major legs and they wanted to let it run for a while.

But the intelligentsia and cultural establishment of Toronto—the opera, ballet, and museum crowd—were a tad miffed by the international coverage this lowbrow story was getting. Wealthy matrons vacationing in Palm Beach were constantly fielding questions not about the Ming pottery exhibit at the ROM or the latest production of the *Ring Cycle* but about the whos, whats, and whys of this damn hockey trophy: "And why the blazes has your team been so bloody dreadful all these years anyway?"

The media were every bit as excited in Quebec as well, but they came at the story from a slightly different angle. "What do you do if you can't win the Stanley Cup? Why, steal it of course." "The Leafs: Slow on their skates but fast with their fingers."

Before long, the tireless investigative work of the reporters from the *Weekly World News* broke the story wide open. They had verifiable reports that the cup had been stolen by aliens and was currently on its way to a colony on the far side of Pluto. Winters on that planet were several decades long, making it very conducive to hockey, and Plutonians felt entitled to their claim on the sport's preeminent trophy. Case closed.

Weeks after the heist, the authorities were still clueless. They searched LaFlamme's palace thoroughly and found nothing. The bartenders and cooks all checked out cleanly. The servers were all young girls hired from a modeling agency, most of whom couldn't even spell *diabolical scheme* let alone plan and execute one.

Because the ransom call had been made from Buffalo, that technically made it an international crime and brought the FBI into the picture. The FBI offered supportive words about the importance of the case and promised every effort would be made to help their Canadian colleagues. The reality, however, was that they had their hands full with Homeland Security, organized crime, and the usual list of murderous wackos. They could ill afford diverting any resources to finding a missing piece of foreign sports memorabilia. They assigned a low-level agent to serve as a token liaison with the RCMP. His job was to make serious-sounding noises, offer profound insights, and give them the impression the FBI had its top people on it.

Even north of the border, the dirty little secret was that police protocol simply didn't warrant giving much attention to this type of crime. As fascinating as the case was, there was no way to justify taking precious resources away from gang wars, drug trafficking, murders, and assaults.

After the initial investigation, the case was assigned to a small task force made up of members of the RCMP, the OPP, and the Toronto police. They would work diligently and follow up on any leads, but there would be no manhunts, no border checks, no search dogs, no SWAT teams.

For a few weeks, the trio wallowed in the bedlam they had caused. They got together nearly every night to flip through the TV news shows and read online commentary. "I borrowed a copy of the *Economist* from one of the people on my route," Zed said one evening. "We're mentioned right after a fascinating article on trade liberalization in the Caucasus region." He gave it to Ian to add to his scrapbook of the best stories and editorials from the major newspapers and magazines.

But as with all news, the story cooled. Eventually, after so many press conferences, interviews, talking heads, and editorials, there was a distinct absence of any new developments. There was no Public Inquiry, the Human Rights Commission would not hear the case, Parliament stubbornly refused to act and naturally the NHL was silent.

It was time, the LJS determined after much deliberation, for round two.

"My friends, there have been shocking new developments in the theft of the Stanley Cup. Just minutes ago, a disk was dropped off at our sister station, CTTR Television." Vaughn Tedesco spoke excitedly. "This video has a short message from the 'kidnappers' and then shows Laurent LaFlamme in what appears to be some sort of coerced confession. We're just going to go ahead and play it right now. Listen carefully."

"I'm Laurent LaFlamme of the Montreal Canadiens. I make this statement of my own free will ..." The audio from his videotaped speech was played in its entirety.

"Now that's not the half of it," Tedesco said when he came back on the air. "He now apparently repeats this little speech in our other official language ... or so it would seem. Listen closely."

The fluently bilingual LaFlamme read the French version of the paragraph.

"Is this patriotic bilingualism in a ransom note? Not on your life!" Tedesco said. "Those of you who speak French will likely have already recognized this. On the surface, it would appear that he simply repeated the statement in our other official language, but he most certainly did not! My guess is that these culprits are afraid of the Quebec language police, as well they should be. Tangling with the OPP and the Mounties is one thing, but the Office Québécois de la Langue Française is another thing altogether.

"I'll read the so-called translation. 'I'm Laurent LaFlamme of the Montreal Canadiens. Two lunatics have broken into my house and are trying to steal the Stanley

Cup. They want me to say some nonsense about awarding it to the Toronto Maple Leafs. They're obviously crazy, but they don't have any weapons and look fairly harmless. One of them is average height, wearing pajamas and a ski mask. The other's quite short, appears to be a body builder and is wearing some type of wetsuit with black gunk all over his face. Both appear to be in their early to mid twenties. I'm just going to read this and hope they leave me alone. Merci.' I am speechless, truly speechless," said Tedesco, clearly anything but.

They were, however, genuinely speechless at the secret lair and world headquarters of the Leaf Justice Squad. Having heard the overdubbed portion of LaFlamme's speech, they went silent. Their faces blanched in unison.

Unfortunately, there had been no budget for translators at the Leaf Justice Squad.

"Those French bastards," Hunter said furiously. "They always figure a way to come back and bite you in the ass."

The speechless Vaughn Tedesco continued his frantic analysis. "So let's consider what's happening here. It's now quite evident that Laurent LaFlamme did *not* wake up to find the cup stolen as he claimed just a few short weeks ago. The video clearly shows him in his living room, reading this ... *confession* ... from a card, wearing some type of bathrobe and standing right beside Lord Stanley's mug.

"What happened in the time between that little speech and the following morning, when the authorities were notified? That's eight or ten hours unaccounted for. How did these two haphazard punks get a big, strong hockey player to do exactly as they wanted? Is there something else going on we don't know about? My senses, my good friends, tell me there is."

Just as it was starting to cool off, the story blazed hotter than ever. It was a near-perfect second act. For the second time in just a few months, Laurent LaFlamme's picture was on the front page of every newspaper in North America. But this second time around, he wasn't shown in video freeze frame receiving an offside pass. This time, he was shown disheveled and glassy eyed in his bathrobe standing beside the stolen trophy.

Once again, Laurent LaFlamme had to do some fancy skating to try to stay onside, but it wasn't the type of skating he was used to. Within an hour of the video's airing, he was on a private plane to New York, having been summoned there posthaste by the league. Less than an hour after landing, he was in front of a press conference at NHL headquarters.

"As it has now become clear," he read from his script in a nervous voice with his French Canadian accent a little stronger than usual, "the information I previously gave regarding the theft of the Stanley Cup ... was not entirely accurate. The two people I described had broken into my home and confronted my fiancée and me late in the evening."

Even though the couple had had no intention whatsoever of getting married, the league spinmeisters had given Suzy a hasty battlefield promotion from girlfriend to betrothed to make his story sound more plausible. The fact was that not only weren't they in love, they didn't even live together. It was a convenient relationship for them both. He had the money and fame she coveted, and she had other obvious assets he coveted, and apparently, he coveted them quite often. But either of them would have moved on in a heartbeat if a better offer came along.

They tried desperately to get in touch with her to give her a heads-up on her impending nuptials, but she was on some remote island in Indonesia doing the year's *Sports Illustrated* swimsuit shoot. She would find out about her unilateral, unannounced engagement only if she saw it on the evening news, which was a long shot. Suzy Sutton didn't make a habit of watching the evening news.

The Flame continued. "Despite their claims of not being violent, after it was recorded, they made physical threats against my fiancée and me. They threatened to do us harm and destroy the trophy if we did not do exactly as they instructed. Because of this, I felt I had no choice but to cooperate. I panicked. I was confused and unsure of what to do. It took me a few hours to gather my emotions and call the police."

Another lie. It had taken him a few hours to sober up and thoroughly get rid of any traces of the cocaine.

"In hindsight, I was obviously wrong and should have had the courage to give the authorities a more precise accounting of the events at the outset. For this I am sincerely sorry and apologize for any confusion my actions may have caused. Thank you."

He turned and hastily walked out of the room going straight into a meeting with his lawyers and the high priests of the NHL. It was time to atone, confess his sins, and receive penance.

There was an obscure clause in the player's collective bargaining agreement to the effect that the league must be informed, briefed, and consulted immediately on all legal matters criminal or civil a player gets involved in regardless of how minor. This literally included things as trivial as parking tickets. "Millionaire Hockey Player parks Ferrari in Handicapped Zone—Refuses to pay $10 Ticket" was the type of newspaper headline the league wanted never to see. All it took was one meter maid given the finger or a bored clerk at city hall to leak it to the press and you have a medium-sized publicity crisis. Players were required to report and provide proof of resolution of any such infraction.

The high priests had heard confessions for hundreds of sins over the years. Bar fights, paternity suits, drunk driving, squabbles with sponsors, shoplifting, fishing without a license, slaps from strippers, unpaid green fees, forged prescriptions, and on and on. It was just another part of the day-to-day operation of any professional sports league.

For the first time since he was a child, LaFlamme was truly, genuinely frightened. As was the case with most professional hockey players, he'd been identified in his early teens as a potential prodigy. That had separated him from the smelly masses of mouth-breathing kids playing the national game and had bought him entry into an exclusive stream of elite teams, specialized training, international competition, and the peripheral privileges unattainable by most teenagers. He'd never had to concern himself with the mundane details of a part-time job, getting spending money, buying a car, or the other major worries of typical high school students. Girls, cars, clothes, cash, and the other accessories of the good life for a talented young man just seemed to materialize out of thin air as needed.

He expected to be heavily fined and suspended or even forced to announce his retirement. The sanctity to say nothing of the financial health of the league was infinitely more important than any one player, even one of his stature. Offering his career as a sacrifice to the ticket-holding, TV-watching, souvenir-buying public was a decision they wouldn't even think twice about.

His glorious and privileged lifestyle, one he had been reveling in since his early teens, could be over. The fat, multiyear contract would be canceled for cause. Sponsorships would vanish. The money would soon dry up after that. Suzy would drop him like a hot stone and simply move on to the next movie star, athlete, or hedge-fund manager salivating at her doorstep. He would probably have to sell at least two of his houses and most of his cars, and worst of all, he would be forced to travel on commercial airlines. Hell, even if he just wanted to watch a game, he'd have to buy his own damn ticket. He'd be a full-fledged, paid-up member of the Sports Hall of Shame right beside Lance Armstrong, Pete Rose, and Ben Johnson.

Sports journalists spent hours pontificating about and debating LaFlamme's massive blunder and trying to decipher what had happened during the missing hours. They speculated on what the NHL play-offs would look like sans trophy. Could they even call it the

Stanley Cup Finals? Corporate sponsors made numerous discreet offers to donate a new trophy filled naturally with millions of dollars. None of the other big four—the NFL, the NBA, or MLB—had yet reduced themselves to selling out to that extent, but the NHL was still the poor sister of the sporting world and was tempted to consider the offers.

However, it wouldn't look right for the winning players to skate around the ice hoisting the Microsoft Trophy. People wouldn't line up in small towns to have their picture taken with the Cialis Cup. Unfortunately, Lord Frederick Arthur Stanley, the sixth governor general of Canada, sixteenth earl of Derby, and lord of Preston, was sadly long gone, and his descendants couldn't be located.

The Leaf Justice Squad continued to hold weekly strategy summits on Friday nights at their global headquarters spending most of their time flipping channels and basking in the chaos they had caused. They were never under the illusion that the result of game seven would actually be overturned, and they were having second thoughts about what exactly they wanted to accomplish. There was no way for them to financially profit from the escapade. They briefly contemplated somehow disguising their return of the cup as a tip and collecting the reward money. But a hundred thousand split three ways simply wasn't worth the risk.

"Besides," said Zed at one of the meetings, "I don't mind being a thieve or extortionist, but I simply will not tolerate being called a liar."

"What's our next move then?" Hunter asked. "We can't just call it a day and give it back. Why don't we sneak it back to the Flame's place? Maybe we could hide it somewhere and make it look like he'd had it stashed there all along. That would really mess him up."

"I like the idea, but it wouldn't work," Zed replied. "The fuzz have already gone through that place with a fine-toothed comb. There'd be no way to get it back there without being detected. Maybe we should just drop it in a locker at the bus depot and call and tell them to pick it up."

Ian had been silent. He had given birth to this adventure and felt responsible to do most of the strategic thinking. They had lost the war but perhaps could win one last battle. They had brought the world's attention to the Canadiens' tainted victory and ensured that it would not go down in history without a significant footnote attached. Laurent LaFlamme's reputation had be damaged beyond repair and there were even solid rumors that he might be traded to Calgary. They took great glee in the thought of LaFlamme, a pure-*laine* Québécois being exiled to the frozen prairie and forced to play in front of a bunch of Alberta rednecks. In some respects, there was nowhere in the known universe farther from urbane, hip Montreal than the cow town of Calgary. And having the Flame actually playing for the Flames showed that the gods of hockey had a not-so-subtle sense of irony. That would most certainly also kill his engagement to Suzy. It was quite unlikely that Suzy Sutton, deity that she was, with a house in Beverly Hills, a co-op in Manhattan, and a *pied-à-terre* in Paris would trade it all for a starter castle in the Alberta foothills. If the rumor was true, that in and of itself made the whole exercise worthwhile regardless of what else they might accomplish.

"We can't go out that easily. We need one final gesture. One last kick at the cat," Ian declared to his fellow conspirators.

"Can we take one last kick at the Habs?" asked Hunter. "There's got to be some way we can stick it to them."

"Stick it to 'em," Zed said, hoisting his glass in salute. "Shove it up their metaphorical asses."

"Thing 'a beauty!" Hunter said, instinctively returning the toast to Zed. "Agreed. Let's go out with a bang."

"Yes," Ian said a few seconds later, staring into space. "Exactly."

Hunter and Zed had seen that look before. They could almost hear the gears turning in his head as his expensive, liberal-arts education bubbled and boiled, congealing into another scheme.

"Let's go out with a bang." He tented his fingers in that annoying gesture and lowered his eyebrows in an evil frown.

"Let's ... go ... out ... with ... a ... bang."

Chapter 8
The *Merde* hits the *Ventilateur*

The Canadiens were scheduled to play their home opener against the Anaheim Ducks at the Bell Center on a Friday evening in early October. That, according to hockey purists, was perfectly representative of what the NHL had been reduced to. Long gone were the glory days of Toronto and Montreal feuding in the cozy confines of the Forum or the Bruins and Rangers grinding it out at Madison Square Gardens. No. That night, the most famous team in hockey would be playing in the phone company's glistening, new, multipurpose, monster-truck, rock-concert, sports-entertainment complex hosting the team from a Los Angeles suburb named after a Disney movie.

Or maybe not.

At eight in the morning the day of the opener, Zed was fully decked out in his invisible superhero cloak of a Canada Post uniform and driving a matching panel truck. He pulled into the nearly empty parking lot of the Bell Center. He unloaded a dolly carrying a large package loosely draped in a plastic sheet. He rolled it toward the center of the lot, took it off the dolly, got back in his truck, and calmly drove away.

In less than half an hour, a stadium employee noticed the box on her way from her car. She decided to investigate. She pulled the sheet off to reveal a large, heavy-duty black case on rollers with the NHL logo and "Property of the National Hockey League" stenciled on it. It looked like *the* sarcophagus. She recognized it from the night it had been awarded to the team four months earlier. The cup had been returned.

Her first instinct was to open it and check inside. But she pulled back. *No*, she thought. *Mustn't touch it. There will be fingerprints and other evidence. Maybe I shouldn't even have touched the plastic cover.* She thought she could be in serious trouble and considered putting the plastic sheet back on. No, she realized. It was too late. The damage had been done. She froze, confused for several seconds before it finally dawned on her to simply call the police.

The first car was there in under sixty seconds. The second came a few seconds after that. Within five minutes, there were a dozen police cars, a fire truck, two ambulances, six news vans, and a helicopter.

Inspector Jean Grenier of the Montreal Police was the ranking officer on duty. Upon getting the news on his radio, he gave strict instructions that the officers were to secure the area but not under any circumstances approach the cup. The significance of this event, he thought, naturally required that a senior officer such as himself step in and manage the situation. It would simply not do to have a junior constable or rookie cop being the one whose picture would undoubtedly be on the night's national news or on the front pages of the next day's newspapers.

Even with the benefit of his unmarked car's sirens and flashing lights, it took him several minutes to get to the parking lot, where twenty-odd police cars, lights flashing, were strategically circling the case. Outside that was a column of news vehicles, everything from the community radio station's small van to the major networks' massive trucks already fully deployed with their satellite dishes pointed skyward ready for an uplink. Two more news helicopters had arrived over the scene. A crowd of bystanders had formed and was quickly growing.

Through his career, Grenier had lamented the fact that he'd had less than his share of glamorous, dramatic policing experiences—major events that found their way into the public eye. He didn't seem to get as many hostage situations, car chases, or grisly murders as he felt he deserved. Those were the biggies that garnered press and interviews and resulted in a little bit of fame and free dinners to boot. All he had ever dealt with were garden-variety homicides, tedious robberies, and unimaginative assaults. He thought this might finally make up for it.

His pulse quickened. He carefully guided his cruiser through the mass of people and drove to the middle of the crowd. When he got out of the car, all eyes turned to him. He instinctively donned his sunglasses as he walked slowly toward the case. After he had taken a few steps, he realized his sunglasses might not make for the best photo. He quickly took them off and stuffed them in his pocket. Another few steps. A voice on his radio summoned him. "Grenier?" He held the radio up to his ear.

"Grenier, this is Leblanc. Hold everything. I'm almost there."

Fabulous, the inspector thought. Chief of Police Michel Leblanc had trumped him and would be taking charge of the crime scene personally. His interviews and free dinners had just evaporated.

Within a few minutes, the chief's Lincoln Navigator, red and blue strobe lights blazing away, arrived. He pulled to a stop, but rather than hopping out right away, he paused, knowing it would take a few seconds for the reporters and photographers to swarm the vehicle. As soon as he felt there was a respectable number of microphones and cameras that would be shortly waving in his face, he emerged with the most serious face he could muster. He feigned disinterest in the reporters' questions. He walked up to Grenier.

Fewer than two blocks away, the magnificent extravaganza's sponsors were watching from the balcony of room 1512 of the Hotel Diplomatique. The executive triumvirate of the Leaf Justice Squad sat comfortably and watched the gala unfold below them. They had reassembled their remote operations center using the same sophisticated surveillance equipment they had used during the first phase of the operation. Hunter and Ian watched through high-powered binoculars while Zed listened to the radio scanner on headphones.

"The guy in the Lincoln is apparently the chief of police," Zed reported. "Sounds like he's going to take charge of the operation. He's talking to that other schmuck in the raincoat."

"Looks at that asshole's uniform," Ian said. "He's only a few tassels shy of being a South American dictator."

The plainclothes officer and his ornately decorated chief strolled around the sarcophagus looking closely and chatting but not touching it. The chief leaned in closer to the case and cocked his head as if trying to hear something. He pulled back, startled. He shouted something to the inspector, who immediately went to his radio.

"Here we go!" Zed reported from under his headphones. "He's called for the canine unit. Wants the bomb squad on standby and the crowd cleared." He continued to relay the radio chatter as the police tried to calmly move the still-growing mob back a safe distance from the suspect case. They poured another round of drinks as they watched the chaotic musical ride going on far below.

First, a large contingent of uniformed officers pushed the crowd back to a radius of about a hundred feet, where they had placed barricades with yellow "Crime Scene" tape. A radio message from the chief to Grenier was pointed. "That frickin' plastic tape isn't going to offer much protection if this thing goes off."

More squad cars were called in. They formed a circle of vehicles end to end. Ian tried to count the vehicles but lost track when he got to a hundred and twenty.

A police van marked "Canine Unit" arrived and was let into the circle. While Grenier and Leblanc stood by, an officer walked a large German shepherd on a short leash to the sarcophagus. The dog was led around it once. It sniffed the box. It sat and looked at its handler, somehow telling him in psychic dog language exactly what was inside.

"Clear the crowd." Zed relayed the chief's orders. "Let's get the bomb squad here ASAP."

"Breaking news out of Montreal this morning," Vaughn Tedesco boomed over the airways. "It's being reported that the Stanley Cup may, and I emphasize *may*, have turned up in of all places the parking lot of the Bell Center, the home of the Canadiens. We have on the line Diane Davis from our affiliate CKMQ in Montreal. Can you describe the scene for us please?"

"Vaughn, there are without exaggeration thousands of people here as well as a few hundred vehicles— police, media, and miscellaneous others as well as a few helicopters buzzing overhead," the reporter said. "But nothing seems to be happening. It's a crime scene after all, and I assume there are certain procedures that must be followed. Evidence needs to be gathered, witnesses interviewed, et cetera. But all the officers just seem to be standing around. Everyone seems to be wondering why they don't just open the case and check inside. It's really quite odd and even sort of eerie."

Chapter 9
Sudden Death

"It's a bomb!" Grenier said in a quiet shout into his cell phone. "It's a goddamn bomb, and his excellency wants me to talk to his majesty about what to do about it."

Grenier was on the phone with Justin Thibault, the executive assistant to Guy Marten, Montreal's mayor. "It's a goddamn bomb. The case is rigged. Put me through to the mayor. Now!"

Thibault had been following the news from the outset on television. It took only a few seconds for him to mentally process the information and realize the ramifications of the situation.

"The dogs confirmed the presence of explosives," the excited inspector said. "The chief noticed some residue and a funny smell when we first checked it out. That's what tipped him off. Nobody knows this yet but you, me, him, and the mutt. We've got a potential mob-scene disaster here if it's not handled properly."

"What's Leblanc doing? Shouldn't he be handling everything?"

"You'd think so, wouldn't you," Grenier said sarcastically. "But apparently, his priority is talking to the reporters. A little scrum has him cornered, and he's milking it for all it's worth."

"That doesn't surprise me, but I still don't see why you're calling the mayor."

"Chief says that he needs him for further instructions," he answered impatiently. "Please put me through *tout de suite.*"

"I don't know where he is—" Thibault was fibbing. "—but I'll track him down ASAP. What exactly do you expect him to do?"

"I have no idea. I'm just playing the secretary. But I'm guessing he needs him to give the bomb squad the go-ahead to neutralize it."

Thibault's extremely sensitive political antennae sprang to attention. "What do you mean *neutralize* it?" he asked even though he already knew the answer.

"We have to set it off.", Grenier confirmed, "We have to blow the bugger up."

Guy Marten was running for reelection and was campaigning in a Montreal suburb. Polls indicated that it was a very tight race; there was less than a week before the vote. He was making small talk and shaking hands at an old folks' home when he noticed the commotion in the TV room. He wandered over to see what was fuss was about. When he realized what was happening downtown, he apologized to his hosts and explained that as mayor, it was imperative that he get to the scene and take charge.

That was nonsense. It was imperative that he get to the scene and cash in on the free publicity. The mayor didn't have any direct role in these matters, but he figured he could at least look as though he were in charge. He could talk to the officers, point randomly at things, yell into a phone, and just generally look mayoral. The news cameras would never know the difference, and it would make great press. Crises, if milked properly, were great for incumbents. Luckily, his cell rang before that could happen.

"Where exactly are you, sir?" Thibault asked.

"I'm on my way to the Bell Center. I should be there. It's a PR jackpot."

"Don't! Do not go within a mile of that place," his assistant insisted.

Marten had a great deal of respect for his right-hand man's instinct and intelligence, so he didn't argue the point. "Why? What's up?"

"It looks like the thing is booby-trapped. They detected explosive residue on the case, and the canine unit confirmed it. This hasn't been made public yet. Leblanc insists on talking to you before he does anything. The only way to deal with these things safely it to set them off. I think he wants to get you to give him the go-ahead to blow it up."

"Can I do that?" he asked, somewhat mystified.

"That's not the point. I think he wants you specifically to give him the order to proceed with the detonation. He doesn't want to be the one responsible for blowing up the Stanley Cup. When he pushes the button, he wants to be able to say he was simply following your orders. Obviously, you don't want to give him those orders."

The mayor understood immediately. Destroying the trophy, an icon deeply woven into the fabric of the city he was trying to govern, wouldn't precisely endear him with the voters in the following week's elections. The polls were close enough without him being made the culprit for this mess. "Got it. Good call. I'm on my way back to the office. You stall him while you can."

Fifteen minutes later, he was at his desk on the phone with Chief Leblanc. They'd had more than a few run-ins over the years on a variety of policing matters. The chief had wanted a police helicopter, but the mayor said there was no room in the budget for that. And after a rash of car thefts, the mayor wanted the police to set up some bait cars to catch the thieves in the act and on video. He'd seen that on American TV and thought it would play well with the public. Leblanc essentially told him to butt out and let them handle it.

Marten thought the chief of police was a sanctimonious blowhard and suspected he was maneuvering his way toward eventually getting his job. Having him lose the election would be a significant step in that direction.

"Michel, what's this I hear about it being rigged?" he asked the chief.

"Our canine unit has confirmed this. There's significant evidence of explosive material in or on the case."

"What kind of explosive material would that be?"

Normally, Chief Leblanc was long winded and loved the sound of his own voice be it in his native French or his flawless English with a quaint Quebecois accent that he could dial up or down depending on the audience. But speaking to his Anglo boss he was suddenly very direct and economical with his speech. "Fertilizer."

"Fertilizer? You kidding me?"

"No sir. Ordinary fertilizer. Ammonium nitrate to be exact. It can be mixed with diesel fuel to make a crude but very effective explosive. The Taliban, Al Qaeda, all them guys, they just love it. Anyone can get the recipe off the Internet. It's cheap, easy, and very effective."

"But you're sure it's an actual bomb? Is it possible that the case wasn't just dragged through someone's barn before it was dropped off?"

"No sir, we're not sure. To be precise, we're never a hundred percent sure that something is an explosive."

"Fair enough. So what would you guess is the probability it's a bomb?"

"I'm sorry, but I can't give you that number, sir. It doesn't work like that. It either is or is not a bomb. You can't say there's a fifty-fifty chance that it is and flip a coin to decide what to do."

"I got ya. So when is this thing supposed to go off?"

"Again, I'm afraid we're not sure. We checked it with a high-sensitivity microphone and other circuit-detection instruments. We don't hear a mechanical clock or detect any electronic circuitry. Of course that doesn't guarantee they're not there. It just means we cannot detect anything."

"It sounds like there's more you don't know than you do know."

The chief didn't respond to this baiting.

"So what would make it go off?"

"It's most likely a simple switch, a very sensitive mechanism that will be triggered when the case is opened or moved."

"Okay, so what do you propose to do next?"

"Standard procedure is to first secure the area. We got lucky there. It's right in the middle of a large open space. There are no tall buildings nearby that might cause secondary damage from falling glass and such. Then we put a ring of concrete highway barriers closer to the device to deflect any blast upward. We're in the process of doing that now as a precaution. Then we place a charge nearby and trigger it by remote control."

"I presume that it's just a small one to set it off? What do you use, blasting caps?"

"On the contrary. We can't risk setting it off and not having all the explosives detonate. It must be large enough to ensure that the explosives in the case fully discharge. There will be a big bang, believe me. It's like hunting a grizzly bear. If you don't kill it with the first shot, you just make things worse."

"Can't you send someone in one of those heavy bombproof suits to disarm it?"

"No sir. That's done only when there's a direct threat to human life. Frankly, we cannot risk an officer's life to save a hockey trophy."

Why don't you put the suit on and go in to disarm it yourself, you blowhole, the mayor thought. *That'll make you a hero.* "What about a robot?"

"We have no robot. Toronto police have a robot, but there's not enough time to get it here."

That was obviously a veiled reference to the helicopter he had been denied. *"Toronto has a robot, but I don't. Toronto has a helicopter. Why can't I have a helicopter?"*

The mayor knew he had to choose his words carefully. "So what are you going to do?"

The chief also chose his words very carefully. "Sir, I suggest that we proceed with the evacuation of the area and detonate the device in the interests of public safety."

"So that's what you're going to do?" the mayor asked.

"Sir, yes, that's my recommendation."

"Your recommendation?"

"Yes sir, that's my recommendation to you, sir."

"That's your recommendation to me? You want me to drive down and set the thing off myself? Isn't that your job?"

"No sir, of course not. It's my official recommendation, as chief of police, that you, as mayor, give orders for the bomb squad to secure the area and detonate the device."

"Why do I have to give the orders?" he asked sarcastically. "Won't they listen to you?"

"It's not that, sir." Leblanc realized that the mayor had caught on to his semantic dance and knew he was trying to put words in his mouth. He had to improvise. "Sir, the policy is that these such ... directions ... in cases like this ... where public safety is involved—" He was rambling and he knew it. "—instructions must come from the head of government."

Instructions must come from the head of government! What the hell's that supposed to mean? Marten smirked. Leblanc was struggling to get out of the very trap he had set for the mayor.

"What exactly do you mean by the head of government?" He was going to probe further.

"Authority ... in cases such as this—" Leblanc continued to flounder. "—are beyond the scope ... of the authority ... due to the nature of the sensitivity ... are beyond the scope of the chief of police."

"Michel, are you trying to tell me blowing things up is not in your job description?"

"Basically, sir, yes I am." He was at least relieved to have one direct answer.

"Well, Michel, I'm not sure it's in mine either. I got elected because I promised inner-city renewal and a bigger snow-plowing budget. You just told me standard procedure was to clear the bystanders and blow the son of a bitch up! Why don't you just go ahead and do that?"

"Yes sir, but—"

"I still don't see how I get involved. It's *your* standard procedure. You know exactly what to do. So why are you talking to me? Why don't you just do it?"

"It's a question of protocol, sir—"

"I see. So now you're telling me procedure and protocol are different things?" He was really twisting the knife in Leblanc's chest. "There was nothing about explosive handling in the oath of office."

"Sir, if you'd allow me to explain." The chief was desperately trying to go on the offensive. "It's standard protocol and accepted police procedure that in situations that are of a sensitive nature, situations that have a potential impact beyond those immediately involved, that the civic government, that is, *you*, be consulted." He had no idea if that was true, but he was fairly sure the mayor didn't either. "This, sir, is clearly one of those situations. Ultimately, Mayor Marten, you're my boss, and it is you to whom I must report." He started to roll. "You delegate me a certain degree of autonomy in handling routine matters, but it would be highly negligent of me to *not* refer matters of such obvious civic importance to you."

In one swift move of verbal kung fu, Leblanc had pulled the knife from his own chest, spun around, and was holding it at the mayor's throat. He was a cop. A battle-hardened, veteran cop. He had stared down gangsters, drug-dealing bikers, and anarchist punks throwing Molotov cocktails without so much as blinking. There wasn't a politician alive that could beat him in a game of liars' chicken. "Having said that, I will do my best to maintain order here and await your decision." He hung up.

The mayor was floored by the chief's swift, elegant rebuttal. He put down the receiver and looked to his assistant. "To be perfectly frank, sir, I'm afraid he's got you. He's spot-on when he says the ultimate authority is with the mayor's office. It's clearly not a provincial or federal jurisdiction, so you can't deflect it their way. And because of the urgency of the situation, you can't exactly call a council meeting and slough it off on them. This, as the saying goes, is why you get the big bucks."

Guy Marten knew better than to argue the point. Justin Thibault knew his stuff cold, and his candor was a valuable asset.

"And with all due respect, we can't sit on this for long." He pointed out the cold, hard facts. "You have a bomb in a parking lot surrounded by thousands of bystanders who have no idea what's in it. That's to say nothing of another twenty thousand who'll be showing up for the game in four hours. Better to blow it up now than risk a bigger disaster."

Marten was leaning back in his chair with his feet on the desk. He was staring at the ceiling. Destroying the Stanley Cup would cost him thousands of votes the following week, but the thought of dozens of people injured or killed was just too horrible to imagine. He had been looking forward to the game himself. He was going to drop the puck at the ceremonial face-off and watch the game from a local construction company's luxury box. Now the election was the least of his problems. If he showed his face within a mile of the arena after this he'd be lynched at center ice right after the national anthems. He would have to think of an excuse to get out of the face-off and would watch from home.

There was no choice. He sat up, pulled his chair to the desk, and picked up the phone. "Go ahead, Michel," he said, closing his eyes and letting out a sigh. "Do what you have to. I'll take full responsibility."

Ten minutes later, Inspector Jean Grenier, despite his vocal protests, begrudgingly followed his chief's direct order. Although he'd had no role in delivering the death sentence, he was the one being forced to pull the lever on the gallows. As instructed, he waited just long enough for the chief to flee the scene in his Navigator before inserting the safety key and turning the switch on the detonator. A loud explosion. The case and its contents were pulverized beyond all recognition.

At long last he had gotten his wish and his moment in the spotlight. He realized he would appear on national TV that night and that tomorrow's papers would have his picture on the front page.

But it was unlikely to get him any free dinners.

"A sad, sad end to the story, my friends. It is a sad day for hockey. It is a sad day for sports. It is a sad day for Canada." Vaughn Tedesco was speaking in his most grave and somber voice, a voice he hadn't used since the collapse of the World Trade Centers and before that the death of Princess Diana. "It's been confirmed by the Montreal police ... that an explosive device was detonated by their bomb squad ... at approximately one-fifteen this afternoon. The case containing the Stanley Cup and allegedly a crude explosive device ... was destroyed this afternoon in the interests of public safety."

The announcer paused for a few seconds of dead air as if to hold himself back from crying.

"In a brief news conference immediately following the detonation, Michel Leblanc, Montreal's chief of police, explained that he had been given a direct order to destroy the case. That order was given by Montreal mayor Guy Marten. As Chief Leblanc explained it, the mayor thought it might contain a bomb and insisted it be detonated immediately rather than considering other options such as attempting to disarm it."

Another even longer pause.

"All that remains of the Stanley Cup is dust and debris, my friends. Shards of history, if you will. All that remains of the Stanley Cup are tiny fragments of silver scattered over a Montreal parking lot. Remnants ... of more than a century ... of history ... and tradition. Ghosts ... of dreams ... and glory."

In the suite of the Hotel Diplomatique, the sponsors of the event were quite satisfied with the result of the day's activity. "With that, gentlemen," Ian declared to the audience of two, "I think we can agree that justice has truly been served. Triumph—" He stood and raised his glass. "—is the domain of the righteous."

Hunter and Zed stood and returned the toast. They drained their glasses in unison and began the job of disassembling their mobile command post and loading the equipment into the Sex Box for the long, quiet ride home.

The lying, cheating, thieving Montreal Canadiens would play their home opener that night in front of twenty thousand mourning fans. The game would be played, most deservedly, under a black cloud.

A very black cloud indeed.

Chapter 10
Silent Night, Holy Grail

In Oakville, Ontario, like many places in the country, the days between Christmas and New Years were somewhat magical. The passage of time seemed to be slowed by the snow on the ground and the frost in the air. Kids were on holiday. Few people went to work, and those who did went in late and left early. It was seven days of no deadlines, eating leftovers, playing with new toys, and wearing new clothes. Everyone stayed up late and slept in. They indulged in everything, including the joy of doing nothing.

John C. Turner Elementary School was adjacent to a sprawling, well-designed urban park with tennis courts, a modern plastic play apparatus, a ball diamond, a soccer pitch, skateboard ramps, an off-leash dog run, and smooth walking paths that weaved between well-kept bluffs of trees. This gem of successful urban planning offered something for everyone.

Despite all the up-to-date amenities, the focal point of the park in the winter was an old-fashioned rink directly behind the school. It had mismatched, partially painted boards topped by a sagging chain-link cage and strings of low-watt, metal, shaded lights overhead.

In an age when recreational hockey had turned into six a.m. practices for the kids and midnight games for adults in modern, heated facilities with cappuccino bars and roomy dressing rooms, the rink was a pleasant throwback to a previous era.

About ten years earlier, during one of the mildest winters in recent memory, a neighborhood tradition had been inadvertently born. Starting at noon on Christmas Day, a big shinny game would spontaneously form. It was a nebulous, organic event in which everyone was welcome to play. It would usually start out with seven or eight players per side, and it would shrink and swell as people came and went. Everyone played—tots, teenagers, twenty-somethings, soccer moms, and single dads.

The unwritten but internationally recognized rules of shinny were strictly adhered to. No skates, no icing, or offsides, no face-offs, and no penalties, and nobody kept score. The number of players on each side would range anywhere from just a few to fourteen or fifteen. It was understood that whenever kids under three played, everyone colluded to set them up and allow them to score a goal. There was at least one fake fight every few hours. The odd time, particularly late at night when the majority of the players were somewhat lubricated, a mock melee would break out. Everyone would throw down gloves and sticks and go around fake punching and pulling each other's sweaters over their heads.

It occasionally turned into a costume party as well. There would be players in Santa Claus outfits or full football gear. Sponge Bob, Roy Rogers, Freddy Krueger, and the Village People all made cameo appearances. One night, there was an entire line made up of Darth Vader and a complement of imperial storm troopers. As might be expected, some fool would occasionally play stark naked save for boots and a toque.

The game lasted for a hundred and seventy hours, seven full days uninterrupted. Once it started that first winter, it just never ended; nobody wanted to go home. That's when the neighborhood tradition began. It ran literally around the clock from Christmas until early in the afternoon on New Year's Day. It went on regardless of conditions or how cold it got. During any bitter cold spells, there would always be a half-dozen or so players dressed in snowmobile suits who would do whatever it took to preserve the continuity.

School-age kids made up most of the players from midmorning on. Parents and family types joined in the afternoon, and university students and shift workers took the graveyard shift. This long stretch was typically fueled with a great deal of rum-laced coffee and variations thereof. Someone with a loud stereo usually backed a car up close to the ice and played loud music from an open trunk.

Police were usually accommodating of the music and the open liquor as long as there were no complaints, which there never were. Once in a while, some of them would even join in the overnight game and play for half an hour in uniform. One officer went as far as to handcuff one of the players during a mock fight and haul him back into his cruiser.

This continued until about nine in the morning, when the grade-schoolers showed up and the process repeated. It was always great fun for everyone involved.

Ian, Hunter, and Zed had played in the early years of the game and had been regular participants since. They usually showed up for the overnight shift and played for a few hours punctuated by warm-up breaks, snacks, and refreshments in the Sex Box, which was always parked nearby.

As might be expected, there was always a big turnout on New Year's Eve. That night, the setting was a picture postcard. It was just a few degrees below zero—not too cold to be uncomfortable but not warm enough to turn the ice and snow to mush. The air was still. It was snowing ever so lightly. The trees were painted with hoarfrost.

At five minutes to midnight, the Leaf Justice Squad initiated what would be the coda of Operation Silver Justice. Ian and Zed were with a handful of other players waiting their turn to get in the game, leaning on the boards near the north end of the rink. Hunter was in the game playing defense for the team on the south side.

His goalie, a middle-aged woman in a purple tracksuit and down vest, stopped a shot and swept the sponge-rubber puck over to him to clear it. Rather than simply passing the puck up the ice, he delicately wedged the tip of his stick underneath it and flipped it up in the air. He perfectly executed a maneuver that he had been practicing diligently over the previous few days. It was supposed to look like an attempt to lob it over everyone and have it land in front of the other team's goal. When executed properly, the move would land the puck near the front of the other team's goal, where hopefully someone would slam it home. This was a commonly used tactic.

However, Hunter muffed the lob, or so it seemed. He sent the puck over everyone's head, over the cage,

111

and into the bluff of trees several yards from the end of the rink.

"I got it," Zed shouted as he turned and trudged into the bush to retrieve the puck. Pucks flew over the boards on a regular basis. The players just paused and caught their breath while someone picked through the snow with his or her stick, dug it out, and tossed it back into play.

"I'll go with you," Ian announced, making sure that at least a few people could hear him. "Make sure you don't hit your head on a branch, you big goof!" He followed him in after the puck.

A minute later, the two of them came out of the bluff side by side, each holding a handle of a large, blue, hockey equipment bag hanging between them. "Look what we found!" Ian shouted so anyone nearby could hear.

"It must have dropped out of Santa's sleigh," Zed said.

"Looks like someone lost his gear," Hunter said loudly.

"Maybe it's a dead body," someone said. "There've been reports of missing drifters in the area."

"I think it's my lunch," another added.

Hunter and Zed continued toward the rink, swung the bag over the boards, and carried it toward the middle of the ice. By then, it had caught most people's attention. A small crowd started circling.

"Be careful. It might be drug money that belongs to the mob," someone warned. "I don't want nuttin' to do with no mob money."

They slid their way onto the rink and set the bag down at center ice. There was a silent pause.

"Open it, you moron!" a smart aleck instructed over the hushed crowd.

"Okay, but if there's any treasure in it, everyone gets an equal share," Ian said. "Agreed?"

He got down on one knee, brushed the snow off, and deliberately, slowly, zipped open the bag. Inside was something wrapped in a worn, plaid, flannel blanket.

He paused a few more seconds trying to let the anticipation build.

"It's the baby Jesus! All rejoice!" someone yelled when he saw the blanket. "Oh come, all ye faithful, joyful and triumphant—"

"That was last week, you idiot," someone said. "Besides, you're thinking of Moses."

"No, I think he's right," another inebriated theologian corrected him. "Moses was in a basket. Jesus was born in a goalie bag."

He carefully lifted it out and laid it on the ice. Pausing for another few seconds to enhance the drama, he reached over and with a slight tremble in his hands unwrapped the blanket.

"I don't believe it!"

"Holy smokes!"

"It can't be! It can't be!"

"This is some kind of a fake. It's gotta be."

"I thought it got blowed up."

While the exclamations and chattering exploded around him, Ian tried to force a surprised look as he stared at the detail of the miraculously resurrected trophy. Hunter and Zed were at the back of the crowd, leaning on the boards, taking it all in with the utmost glee. They sported huge grins, and at one point they almost hugged, but restrained themselves at the last second. Nobody was paying them the least bit of attention.

"No, look." Ian pointed to the engraving. "Look at the detail. It's too good to be a fake. It's too old to be a fake. It's the real thing! It's the Stanley frickin' Cup!" He had never used the word *frickin'* before in his life. He was going to use the other F word but reflexively caught himself at the last second when he remembered all the children nearby. "It's the Stanley goddamn effin' Cup!"

As spontaneous as he could make it look, he hoisted it over his head, exactly like the players did, one hand on the base and the other on the lip. He slid in a big circle around the ice, skating in his running shoes. He shouted and screamed at the top of lungs. He wasn't acting. It was genuine. It was his victory. It was justice for his beloved Leafs. It was the culmination of a plan conceived, designed, and executed perfectly. If he had died right then and there, he would have done so a happy man. His was the ultimate triumph of the righteous.

The crowd was euphoric. For all they cared, Ian Andrews might just as well have scored the winning goal in sudden death of game seven. The crowd couldn't have been more elated even if it had actually been the resurrected baby Jesus swaddled in a smelly hockey bag.

After his victory lap, Ian went to the spot where the other two were standing, smiling and as ecstatic as he was. He passed it to Hunter, who, never being one to miss a chance to show off his upper-body definition, had already stripped down to his tightest, sleeveless Leaf T-shirt. He did his lap pumping the cup in the air and screaming at the top of his lungs, "Take that, you frickin' Canadien bastards!" subconsciously copying Ian's lead on the *F* word. He went to hand it off to Zed, and when he saw Zed's face, he nearly fell over.

Zed was crying. The freakishly tall, long-haired, underachieving, stoic, hippie postman was standing there with tears in his eyes. Not just watery eyes, mind you, but full-flowing, salty tears running down both cheeks.

"Cheer up, Zeddy!" Hunter screamed over the roar of the crowd and gave him a huge slap on the back as he started his lap.

But Zed went only a few steps before he slid to a stop. As gangly as he was on the ice at the best of times, he knew that with all this emotional excitement, he could easily fall and break one of his legs. Or the trophy. He just stood there, soaking in the moment, pumping the trophy high over his head, and turning in a full circle to show everyone. After he gathered his composure, he brought it down to his lips and gave it a long, slow kiss. He looked through the crowd for the smallest child he could find. He went over and gave it to her.

The small girl in a pink snowsuit was only a few inches taller than the trophy. She had no idea what was going on or the significance of the event, She tried lifting it but it was too heavy so she also gave it a kiss and pushed it over to her mom. Mom picked it up with a bit of effort, gave it a tiny peck and passed it off to the next person, and so on. The ecstasy continued for the next half hour. It turned in to a spontaneous reenactment of the real postgame, on-ice celebration with everything but the speeches from the owners and league president.

While the few dozen people at the rink were waiting their turn with the trophy, the Leaf Justice Squad quietly retreated to the Sex Box in the school parking lot. Zed started the engine and revved it a few times to warm it up. Hunter sat silently in the passenger seat watching the crowd through the van's slightly fogged windshield. Ian retrieved a bottle of champagne from the small fridge in the back and perched himself between the two front seats. He popped the cork, took a few large gulps, and passed it around to the other two.

With the frost in the air and a low blanket of clouds backlit by a full moon, midnight glowed in soft focus under the lights of the rickety community rink. As the motor hummed and the van warmed up, the justice trio watched silently while everyone on the ice took a victory lap with the Stanley Cup. The cup they, with their very own hands and guided by the gods of hockey, had valiantly rescued.

"Thing 'a beauty," Hunter whispered. "Thing 'a beauty."

A few days later, the cup had been safely returned to its permanent home at the Hockey Hall of Fame in downtown Toronto. The curator, giving the trophy its regular polishing, was taking much longer than he normally did, spending extra time shining it over and over. The whole incident had been something of a nightmare for him as well. Rubbing the cup with a soft, cotton cloth was quite therapeutic. He almost talked to it as if he had been reunited with a lost child.

While reading the ring freshly engraved with the names of that year's winners, he thought he saw a minor imperfection in the silver plaque. He couldn't make it out clearly even with his strong reading glasses. He went to his desk and retrieved a large magnifying glass for a closer look.

At first he thought it was a scratch or dent. It was almost microscopically small, but it was unmistakable nonetheless. On the inscription, beside the name of Laurent LaFlamme, was a minute but skillfully etched, teensy, tiny mark. It was unmistakable. Quite clear despite its size. He stared at it for a few seconds. A smile slowly came across his face.

Like angels metaphorically dancing on the head of a pin it succinctly summed up the pure karma and divine justice of this entire escapade. It was a diabolical pinprick of genius that would punctuate the history of this iconic trophy for all time.

It was absolutely perfect.

It was an asterisk.

The End

CPSIA information can be obtained at www.ICGtesting.com
Printed in the USA
LVOW10s2225271115

464076LV00001B/10/P